D1039956

STOLEN IDENTITY

HARDY BOYS ADVENTURES

#16 *STOLEN IDENTITY*

FRANKLIN W. DIXON

ALADDIN   New York London Toronto Sydney New Delhi

ALADDIN
An imprint of Simon & Schuster Children's Publishing Division
1230 Avenue of the Americas, New York, NY 10020
First Aladdin paperback edition February 2018
Text copyright © 2018 by Simon & Schuster, Inc.
Cover illustration copyright © 2018 by Kevin Keele
THE HARDY BOYS MYSTERY SERIES, HARDY BOYS ADVENTURES,
and related logos are trademarks of Simon & Schuster, Inc.
Also available in an Aladdin hardcover edition.
All rights reserved, including the right of reproduction in whole or in part in any form.
ALADDIN and related logo are registered trademarks of Simon & Schuster, Inc.
For information about special discounts for bulk purchases, please contact Simon & Schuster
Special Sales at 1-866-506-1949 or business@simonandschuster.com.
The Simon & Schuster Speakers Bureau can bring authors to your live event.
For more information or to book an event contact the Simon & Schuster Speakers Bureau
at 1-866-248-3049 or visit our website at www.simonspeakers.com.
Series designed by Karin Paprocki
Interior designed by Mike Rosamilia
The text of this book was set in Adobe Caslon Pro.
Manufactured in the United States of America 0118 OFF
2 4 6 8 10 9 7 5 3 1
Library of Congress Control Number 2017942662
ISBN 978-1-4814-9967-5 (hc)
ISBN 978-1-4814-9966-8 (pbk)
ISBN 978-1-4814-9968-2 (eBook)

CONTENTS

OFF WITH A WARNING

1

FRANK

"YOU GOING TO FINISH THAT?" JOE ASKED as he snatched the last piece of bacon from my plate.

"Yes," I replied, resisting the urge to jab my brother's hand with my fork. "I was."

"Don't quarrel, boys," Aunt Trudy said as she placed another plate of bacon onto the table. "There's plenty to go around."

I replaced the stolen strip of bacon and went back to my open chemistry book. Wednesday was always "pop quiz" day in Mr. Watson's class. Although no one understand why he called it a "pop" quiz when it consistently occurred on the same day every week.

"Hey, bro," said Joe. "It was just a piece of bacon. You didn't have to call the cops on me."

I looked up to see my brother staring out the kitchen window. We watched a police cruiser slow to a stop in front of our house.

"I wonder what's up," I muttered.

The driver's door opened and a uniformed officer—a tall woman I didn't recognize—stepped out and strode up our sidewalk toward our front door.

I raised an eyebrow at Joe. "What did you do?"

"Oh, sure. Blame me," replied Joe.

I was just messing with my brother. We may be known around town for our sleuthing, but we'd never received unannounced police house calls before.

The doorbell rang and Aunt Trudy turned to us. "I'll go see what this is about. You boys finish your breakfast, it's almost time to get going." She tossed her dish towel down and went to open the front door.

Joe and I put our forks down so we could listen in. The police officer's voice was muffled but Aunt Trudy's came through loud and clear.

"They're overseas right now," we heard Aunt Trudy say. The officer must've asked about our parents. "Fenton stayed over after his detectives' conference, and Laura flew out to meet him. She wasn't going to let him enjoy Paris all by himself!"

There was laughter from the officer and then more words I couldn't quite make out.

"Oh, the boys are in here," said Aunt Trudy, her voice getting louder. "They haven't left for school yet."

Aunt Trudy led the officer into the kitchen. The woman had a folded newspaper under one arm.

"Boys, this is Lieutenant Wolfe," said Aunt Trudy. "She's here to talk to you." Our aunt turned to the lieutenant. "Can I get you some coffee?"

The woman smiled. "No thank you. I won't be too long." She took a seat at the table. "I just need to speak to Frank and Joe about a small police matter."

Aunt Trudy beamed. "Ooh, another case. I'm sure the boys will be as helpful as always." She grabbed her own coffee mug and headed for the living room. "I'll leave you to it, then."

I turned back to the lieutenant, who was no longer smiling.

"Hello, boys," she greeted us. "I just transferred over a couple of months ago. We haven't crossed paths yet, but I've heard an awful lot about you."

Joe grinned. "Our reputation precedes us, huh?" he asked. "Hey!"

I had kicked my brother under the table. Something told me this was not just a friendly get to know the neighborhood visit.

"Is there something we can help you with?" I asked politely.

The lieutenant didn't answer right away. She just stared

at me from across the table. I finally broke eye contact and glanced at Joe. He simply shrugged.

"I picked up your newspaper outside," said the lieutenant. She pulled out the paper out from under her arm and held it up for us to see.

"That's our dad's," said Joe. "He still likes his news old-school." My brother held up his phone. "Not like us."

The woman pursed her lips and carefully unfolded the paper to reveal the front page. "How about I read an article for you . . . old-school."

"You came over here just to read us the newspaper?" I asked.

Lieutenant Wolfe shrugged. "Why not? I'm a public servant, after all."

She cleared her throat before she began reading "'Local Teenagers Assist Baffled Bayport PD.'"

I cringed and stole a glance at Joe. His face mirrored mine. This wasn't going to be good.

After a quick look in our direction, the lieutenant read past the headline. "'Terrance Harlow was taken into custody yesterday by state police and is due to be transferred back to Bayport to face criminal indictment. He is charged with masterminding the string of home burglaries that plagued Bayport suburbs last month. Using a landscaping business as a cover, Harlow allegedly broke into houses and stole jewelry while homeowners were at work. However, it wasn't the hard work of Bayport's finest that led to his plot being uncovered.

Instead Harlow was identified by the sleuthing skills of two Bayport High students—Frank and Joe Hardy.'"

"I don't know how the paper found out about that," I said. "We didn't talk to the press." I looked at Joe. "Did we?"

Joe ran a hand through his blond hair and looked up at the ceiling. He didn't answer.

"I'm not finished," Lieutenant Wolfe said through tight lips. She looked back down at the paper. "'Our big break in the case came when we realized that most of the burglaries were just a cover,' said Joe Hardy. 'Harlow was really after a diamond necklace that had been willed to his niece. He thought it rightfully belonged to him. He thought the theft wouldn't be traced back to him if it was just one of many.'"

"I didn't know she was a reporter," explained Joe. He half smiled. "At first."

"Oh, and you didn't stop there," said the lieutenant. She read more. "'"We solve cases for the police all the time," Joe Hardy went on to say. "My brother and I have been doing it since we were little kids. You could even say mystery solving is in our blood. Our father, Fenton Hardy, is a renowned detective."'"

"You were flirting," I accused my brother. "Flirting and bragging."

Joe just shrugged.

Lieutenant Wolfe cleared her throat and continued reading. "'Police Chief Olaf is on extended leave and could not be reached for comment. However, Lieutenant Patricia

Wolfe was brought in to lead the department in his absence. One concerned citizen, who didn't wish to be named, had this to say: "I don't know who this Wolfe lady is, but I'm glad the Hardy Boys are still around to pick up the slack while Olaf is gone."'"

I cringed and Joe sucked in a breath after hearing the last line.

The lieutenant read on. "'The Bayport Police Department did not comment directly, but Lieutenant Wolfe's office released the following statement: "While we appreciate citizens keeping watch for criminal activity, the Bayport Police Department does not condone vigilantism in any form whatsoever."'"

"Vigilantes?" I asked. "That seems a little strong."

Lieutenant Wolfe folded the paper. "Not in my book." She tossed the paper onto the table. "Do you know what kind of grief I'm going to get when the chief finds out about this?"

"Don't worry about the chief! He's used to us helping out. He comes off all scary, but he's really just a big teddy bear once you get to know him," Joe said with smile, clearly hoping his explanation would make this all go away.

I shook my head. "Why is the chief on extended leave?"

"His mother is ill and he took time off to care for her," the lieutenant replied.

"We're sorry to hear that," I said. "And look, we didn't mean for you or the police to look bad in that article." I shot a brief look to Joe. "We just try to help when we can. We always try to work with the police. Not undermine them. This is really just a misunderstanding."

The woman leaned forward. "You're teenagers. The Bayport police department does not need your help. I checked with the other officers, and it seems you two have been given a lot of leeway with your detecting hobby. But I don't care who your father is. It's dangerous and I won't stand for it. You leave the mysteries and crime fighting to the police." She pointed a long finger at each of us. "In fact, if I see you as much as handing out a missing pet flyer, I'm detaining the both of you for questioning."

I raised both hands. "The only mystery on my mind right now is how to pass my chemistry quiz."

The lieutenant got to her feet. "Glad to hear it." She glanced at her watch. "About time you got to school, isn't it? You need a ride?"

"Frank has a car," Joe volunteered.

"Oh, yeah." The lieutenant smiled as she pulled out her phone. She tapped the screen a few times and proceeded to rattle off the make and model of my car, the date it was purchased, the purchase price, its license plate number, and . . . "A parking violation last fall."

Joe raised a hand. "Uh, that was me."

She put her phone away. "Well, as soon as I get back to the station, every officer is going to have this information with orders to keep a watchful eye on both of you." She gave a sly smile. "I wouldn't roll through any stop signs if I were you."

The lieutenant's smile disappeared, and she strode out of the kitchen and left our house. Joe and I watched through the window as she climbed into her squad car and drove away.

"She was kind of intense, huh?" asked Joe.

I nodded as I checked my watch. "Oh, man. We're going to be late." I closed my textbook and shoved it into my backpack. "Especially since I'll have to drive five miles under the speed limit, thanks to your big mouth."

"Hey, we've gotten press before," said Joe.

"Not making the police look bad like that," I pointed out. "And not when Olaf was out of town. He's established and not trying to prove anything. This is a pretty big deal for a new lieutenant. No wonder she's mad." I moved my plate to the sink.

"Yeah, you're right. I definitely could've phrased things a little better."

"You think?"

"Well how was I supposed to know Olaf was going to be gone! Anyway, I'm sure it'll all blow over."

"Agreed. But we better do what she says for the next couple of weeks. No cases, no mysteries, nothing out of the ordinary."

Joe smiled. "Well, after tonight, right?"

Oh, man. I'd completely forgotten about tonight.

A PAGE FROM HISTORY

2

JOE

I T WAS ALL I COULD DO TO TALK FRANK INTO going out that night as planned. After our visit from Lieutenant Wolfe, my brother had tried to back out several times throughout the day. I had to catch him between classes and talk him into it all over again . . . and again and again. I had to remind him that this was his idea in the first place.

"Better park in the back," I said as we drove closer to the museum that evening.

Frank drove past the large building and turned down a small side street, remembering to signal several feet before the turn. We hadn't seen any police cars along the way, but Frank had still been overly cautious about obeying traffic laws.

He shot me a look. "If there's nothing wrong with what we're doing, then why should I park in the back?"

"Better safe than sorry," I replied with a shrug.

Frank tightened his lips and gave me that look that said he might try to back out again.

"Hey, a museum employee is letting us inside," I said. "It's all good. Now, *he* might be breaking some rules, but not us."

Frank made another turn and we coasted down the large alley behind the museum. When we reached the museum's loading dock, I pointed to a white van in a small parking lot across the alley. "Ooh, park behind that van."

"You mean *hide* the car behind the van," Frank corrected.

"Might as well be careful, huh?"

Frank pulled behind the van and killed the engine. We got out and walked across the lot toward the museum.

As we neared the loading dock, Frank grabbed my arm and stopped. "Check it out."

I followed his gaze to a pair of legs poking out of a pile of trash against the building.

"Is that . . . ?" My voice trailed off. We changed course and moved cautiously to what looked like a poorly hidden dead body.

But the mystery was solved as quickly as it was discovered. A homeless man had created a makeshift shelter for the night. What looked like a pile of trash was actually a collection of items loaded onto an old wheelchair—clearly the man's personal possessions.

"Oh, I see—" I began.

Frank shushed me and held a finger to his lips, instructing me not to wake the man. We each pulled out our wallets and placed some bills into an empty coffee cup in front of the sleeping figure. He didn't stir as we backed away and headed back toward the museum.

We climbed the steps leading to a door beside the large loading dock. Frank took out his phone and sent a text. A minute later and a familiar face poked through the door.

"About time you got here," said our friend Hector Cruz. "Come on in."

We entered a large open area full of wooden crates, carts, and a forklift. It was like a scene out of *Raiders of the Lost Ark*, like there could be a mysteriously dangerous artifact hiding among the packing. I sent a silent wish to the stars that nothing out of the ordinary would happen this evening. My brother and I don't have the best track record when it comes to avoiding mysteries . . . or danger.

"I take it this isn't on the usual tour," I said.

"There's no one else here, is there?" asked Frank.

Hector smiled. "Just us." He headed across the loading area. "This way," he said. "Shortcut."

Frank and I followed Hector through a plain door and entered the museum itself. We found ourselves surrounded by fossilized dinosaur skeletons, glass encased dioramas, and giant murals of grassy landscapes. Frank and I had been visiting the Bayport Museum since we were little kids. Between school field trips and weekend family visits, we knew our way around fairly well. Hector was leading us through the dinosaur exhibit toward the gallery set aside for traveling exhibits.

We passed through a hallway and approached an entrance with a banner reading A CENTURY OF SOLVING CRIME.

Hector flipped on the lights and dramatically spun around. He walked backward through the entrance with his arms opened wide, gesturing at the room around us. "Am I a great friend or what?" he asked. "As promised, a sneak peek at tomorrow's new exhibit."

The hall was filled with displays featuring everything from giant DNA sequences to a booth about Sir William James Herschel and Sir Francis Galton, the first people to use fingerprints for identification. But neither of those attractions were what interested us most. Hector led us to an open book resting on a pedestal in the center of the gallery. A spotlight hung above it and red velvet ropes fenced it off from the rest of the room. Clearly, this was the main attraction. The book was an original handwritten bound manuscript by Sir Arthur Conan Doyle himself, the creator of the greatest fictional detective of all time: Sherlock Holmes.

Of course, Frank and I were huge Sherlock Holmes fans. Frank a bit more than me, actually. Both of us grew up reading all the Holmes stories and books. We've seen all the movies and television shows based on the character. What detective wouldn't be a fan of the world's greatest detective, even he was fictional?

Hector unclipped one of the velvet ropes. "Come on up and take a look," he suggested. "VIP tour."

Frank and I stepped up to the book. It was opened to the first yellowed page. The author's cursive handwriting was clear under the spotlight. The title of the story spread across the top of the page: "A Scandal of Bohemia." The story began right under the title.

"Is this a good one?" asked Hector. "I've never read any Sherlock Holmes stories."

"It's not the most famous one," Frank replied.

"Yeah, that's more like 'The Hound of the Baskervilles,'" I added.

"But it's one of my favorites," Frank continued. "It was the first Holmes story to be published in the *Strand Magazine* back in 1891. There it was retitled 'A Scandal *in* Bohemia.'"

Yeah, Frank was *way* more of a Sherlock Holmes fanboy than I was.

"It gets better," said Hector. He dug into his pockets and pulled out two pairs of white cotton gloves. "If you want to *carefully* look through it, you have to wear these."

He handed us the gloves. Frank slipped his on with lightning speed and began to gently turn the first page.

"Seriously, though, be careful," warned Hector. "Josh said it was on loan from some university in Texas."

"Who's Josh?" I asked as I put on my pair of gloves.

"Josh Jenkins. He's the assistant director in charge of this exhibit," replied Hector. "And my boss."

"And he's okay with this?" I asked. "Us coming here?"

Hector looked at me like I was crazy. "Heck, no. He doesn't know you're here. But I knew you guys would love this thing and not mess it up." He shrugged. "Besides, it was kind of Josh's idea. He told me that anyone who loved a mystery would be thrilled to see this in person. So naturally, I thought of you guys."

"You rock, Hector," I said, giving him a fist bump.

Hector smiled. "I know."

I moved closer to get a turn at the manuscript. "You know we don't have time for you to read the entire thing, bro."

"I've read it already," Frank said, not looking up from the pages.

"Of course you've read it," Hector said. "I'm sure you guys have read all the Sherlock Holmes stories tons of times."

"No, I mean I've read this particular manuscript," Frank explained. "The university scanned in the pages and uploaded them to their website."

Hector shook his head in disbelief. "Then why am I risking my new job to show you this?"

"Because you're a great friend," I replied, patting him on the shoulder. "Remember?"

Frank carefully flipped another page. "Because seeing this in real life, turning the actual pages, that's way better." He turned another page. "It's a connection to the author himself. It's like touching history."

Hector leaned over Frank's shoulder. "Wait, that's different handwriting. Is this a fake or something?"

Frank shook his head and turned another page. "Parts of the manuscript were written by Doyle's secretary."

"Of course you know that," I chuckled.

Frank tried to turn the next page but it pulled away from the book. It wasn't bound like the others. "Uh-oh," he said as the loose page dangled between two fingers.

"Oh, man!" Hector's eyes widened. "What did you do, Frank?"

My brother shook his head. "I didn't do anything. It was already loose." He gingerly set the page beside the open book. Then he placed a finger onto the next page. With the slightest effort, that page pulled away from the binding. "This one is loose too."

"Dude, stop ripping pages out of the book!" Hector ordered.

"They were never attached to begin with," Frank explained. "Are they supposed to be like that?"

"I don't know," replied Hector. "I never touched the thing." He buried his face in his hands. "This was a bad idea. I am so fired."

Something seemed weird about the loose pages. I leaned in for a closer look. "The paper color doesn't quite match the rest of the pages, does it?"

Frank turned to one of the attached pages and laid the loose page over it. The loose page was yellowed like the others, but not quite the same shade. It was lighter.

I reached into my pocket and pulled out my retractable magnifying glass and pulled the loose page aside. I carefully examined the writing. It was completely flat. When I zoomed in on the writing on the attached page, the ink was raised, ever so slightly.

"I don't think this page is part of the original manuscript," I reported. "I think it's a forgery."

Frank had pulled several more loose pages away from the binding. He ran a finger along the inside seam of the book. "I can feel several thin edges here," he said. "I think the original pages were cut out."

"So someone stole pages from Doyle's manuscript?" I asked.

GROUND ZERO 3

FRANK

WHO ARE YOU TWO?" LIEUTENANT Wolfe asked as she approached Joe and me. She hadn't stopped glaring at us since the police had arrived at the museum. "You *look* like Frank and Joe Hardy, but you can't be them." She shook her head. "Oh, no. Because I told those boys, just this morning, in fact, that I didn't want to see them near any investigation of any kind."

"We're not investigating," Joe explained. "We're witnesses."

"Witnesses who happen to be in a museum after hours," she added.

Joe opened his mouth to reply, but I nudged him with my elbow. Luckily, one of the many police officers took her aside to report his findings.

Joe, Hector, and I had decided to call Hector's boss first. Josh Jenkins wasted no time getting to the museum and confirming that the manuscript pages in question were indeed forgeries. Josh had insisted that we stick around while he called the police. Wearing his own set of white cotton gloves, he continued to study the manuscript while Lieutenant Wolfe and several other officers searched the museum for signs of a break-in.

Josh was tall and thin. He had dirty-blond hair and one of those faces that made him seem younger than he probably was. He looked more like one of our friends than an assistant director of a museum.

Lieutenant Wolfe held out an open palm toward me. "I need your car keys and consent to search your vehicle."

"You want to search my car?" I asked.

"I have probable cause," Wolfe replied. "With you two being here . . . well, let's just say that I don't believe in coincidences. Plus, it's in your best interest to cooperate."

"Fine," I sighed. "But it's already open. The rear passenger door doesn't lock." I glared at my brother. The last time he borrowed my car, one of his friends shut the door on a hockey stick. Both the stick and the door latch broke in the process.

Joe raised his hands. "I really am saving up to get it fixed. Promise."

Wolfe nodded to one of the officers. He marched to the back of the museum, no doubt to give my car the once-over.

"Look, Lieutenant, we're just Sherlock Holmes fans," I explained. "That's all."

"It's true," agreed Hector. "That's why I invited them to see the manuscript."

The woman crossed her arms. "Big enough fans to take a little souvenir?"

"If we stole the pages, we wouldn't have called Hector's boss when we discovered the forged pages."

"That makes sense," said Josh. He took off his gloves and joined us. "Although I'm not happy about them being here, I'm glad they let me know about the theft."

"Are you sure that the manuscript didn't just come that way?" Joe asked. "Maybe the university lost the pages a long time ago."

Lieutenant Wolfe's eyes widened. "Excuse me." She rounded on my brother. "I know you just didn't ask him an investigative question. As if you were a detective on this case."

Joe cringed. "Uh, I guess not."

"Well, whoever asked," said Josh, "for the record, I did check every page when the manuscript arrived. It's all part of the job."

"Every single page?" asked the lieutenant.

"I read the entire thing," replied Josh. He nodded at Joe and me. "I'm a big Sherlock Holmes fan too."

The lieutenant sighed. "All right, we'll keep searching the museum for signs of a break-in or a stash spot for the pages." She glanced down at her phone. "Hector Cruz, I'll need to speak to you some more."

"Me too," agreed Josh.

The officer who'd been sent to check out Frank's car walked up to Wolfe. "Lieutenant, the car was clean," he reported. "No sign of any manuscript pages."

"Hardy brothers, go home," Wolfe ordered. "Your part as 'witnesses' for this investigation is over . . . for now. And I don't want a word of this to end up in tomorrow's paper. We're keeping this quiet for now." She eyed Joe in particular. "Understood?"

Joe nodded. "Of course."

"And one more thing." She leaned forward. "The Bayport Police Department does not need your help. Remember that."

"Yes, ma'am," I said.

She nodded. "Good answer. But if I find out that you're investigating this case . . . well, let's just say that I can get a couple of material witness warrants real quick. I can hold you in a cell for questioning for . . . well, who knows how long."

One of the officers walked us out of the front of the museum. We had to walk around the entire building to get to my car. When we reached the back, I noticed that the homeless man and his stash were gone. Either the police presence scared him off or they had him simply move along to a shelter. The white van was gone too, leaving my car easy for the police to spot (and search). Joe and I climbed in without a word and drove for home.

"What if—" Joe began.

"Don't start," I warned. "You heard what she said."

"Yeah, sure," Joe said. "But we were right there at the scene of the crime. Ground zero."

My brother was right. My mind was already buzzing with questions about scenarios, suspects, and motives. Sherlock Holmes and his partner, Dr. Watson, wouldn't hesitate if a mystery landed in their lap like this.

"You know what Holmes would say right now?" Joe asked, practically reading my mind.

I smiled. "The game is afoot."

"That's right," agreed Joe. "And it is!"

"It may be," I said. "But you heard what the lieutenant said. We can't investigate anything if we're stuck in jail. I don't think she was joking about those material witness warrants."

"Yeah, she seemed pretty serious," said Joe. "That newspaper article really got under her skin."

"Look, let's sleep on it," I suggested. "We can talk to Hector tomorrow at school, but that's it for now. Deal?"

"Deal," agreed Joe.

We didn't speak for the rest of the way home. But if I know my brother, his mind was in overdrive, working all the angles of the case. I know mine was.

I pulled into the driveway and killed the engine. As we climbed out, I noticed something in the backseat.

"You left stuff in my car again," I told my brother.

"No, I didn't," Joe replied.

"Backseat." I tapped the rear window.

Joe peered through to see the sheet of paper. "It's not mine."

I shook my head and laughed as I opened the back door. I didn't notice the page's yellow tint under my dim dome light. But a chill ran down my spine when I picked it up and got a closer look. I turned it over to see familiar handwriting on the other side.

"Oh, man," I muttered.

Joe jogged around the car to see what I held. His eyes widened when he caught a glimpse.

"Dude," he said.

It was one of the missing manuscript pages.

UNEXPECTED GIFT

4

JOE

"MAYBE HECTOR SET US UP," FRANK suggested as he drove us to school the next day. "You know, as a prank."

"Almost getting us arrested is a pretty big prank. And not a very good one," I said.

"Well, he didn't know about our morning visit from Lieutenant Wolfe," said Frank. "So he wouldn't know it would get us in so deep, so quickly."

That was true. Frank and I had decided to keep that little conversation to ourselves. Otherwise, our friends would never let us hear the end of it.

"I don't think it was Hector," I said. "First: he wouldn't have called his boss. Second: how could he slip the missing page into your car? He was with us the entire time."

"And the cops searched my car," Frank said with a scowl. I could tell he didn't like the idea of them going through his property. "The page had to have been left *after* the search."

"Think it was one of the officers?" I asked. "They could've planted it."

"I can't see any of the Bayport police planting evidence," replied Frank. "And even if they did, what would be the motive? Why say that the car was clean when they could've arrested us on the spot?"

"Or stopped us on the way home," I added.

"Right," Frank agreed as he turned into the school parking lot. He pulled to a stop and climbed out.

I had been trying to talk Frank into going into full investigation mode, no matter what the lieutenant said. With the missing page in our possession, I didn't see any other options.

"Okay, you have to admit it," I said as I followed Frank across the parking lot. "We're in the middle of this now. We *have* to investigate."

Frank sighed. "Yeah, I hear you." He held up a finger. "But we have to keep an ultra-low profile. Lower than ever before."

"Hey, I don't want to be stuck in a holding cell any more than you do," I said. "I have a track meet Saturday, remember?"

My brother and I *had* discussed the case a bit the night before. We had discussed turning the page over to the police. Chief Olaf might've believed the page was planted on us, but Lieutenant Wolfe? Extremely doubtful.

We also tried to guess why someone would steal only a few pages from the valuable manuscript. Frank had pulled up the university's website, and we looked over the scanned versions of the missing pages. Although the author had made some notes in the margins of a few of the pages, there was nothing important scribbled on the pages in question; no secret codes, no clues to long-lost treasure. I even tried putting the original page under a black light to see if there was anything written in a secret ink. I *almost* brushed it in lemon juice but Frank wouldn't let me. We searched online for a legend that would connect the pages with some bigger plan but couldn't find anything. There didn't seem to be anything relevant in the story, either. The pages seemed to be cut out at random.

No, this seemed to be more about framing us than getting anything out of those pages. And there was no shortage of criminals who would want revenge. The only question was, which one was it?

Frank and I split up and headed for our first-period classes. Luckily, I sat beside Hector in mine. It was up to me to begin the investigation—carefully.

I went into history class and slid into my desk. Hector was already at his.

"Hey," I said.

"Don't 'hey' me, man," Hector growled. "Not after last night."

"You invited us, remember?" I asked.

Hector dropped his head. "I know. I'm more mad at myself than you guys. I should've just let you look at the book behind ropes like everyone else."

"So what happened last night, after we left?" I asked.

"I got fired, that's what happened," Hector said.

"Dude, I'm sorry about that," I said. I wasn't totally surprised, but it was still a bummer.

"It's not your fault," Hector said, shaking his head. "Of course, I only got fired after I told the story to the police three more times."

"Common tactic," I said. "They wanted to see if your story matched each time."

"Oh, yeah, Mr. Detective . . ." Hector reached into his backpack and pulled out a business card. "I'm supposed to call Lieutenant Wolfe if you or Frank ask me any questions."

"You're not going to, are you?" I asked.

He smiled and put the card away. "No, don't worry. But she doesn't like you two for some reason. What did you do to tick her off?"

"It's a long story," I said. "But sorry again about your job."

"It was such a sweet gig, too." Hector sighed. "I practically stumbled on it in the first place. And Josh was the best boss I ever had. I basically got paid for hanging out and shooting the breeze with him. Now I gotta see if they're hiring at the Meet Locker."

The bell rang, sounding the end of our conversation and

the beginning of class. For the next fifty minutes, I learned more than I ever wanted to know about Samuel Adams, Paul Revere, and the whole rowdy gang.

After class, I swung by my locker to exchange books. I'd catch up with Frank later and tell him about the lieutenant asking Hector to snitch on us. I dialed my combination and swung open the door. An envelope rested atop the pile of books and other various junk inside my locker. Someone must have slipped it through the vents in the locker door. Maybe Frank had come up with something about the case that couldn't wait. I opened the blank envelope, and my eyes widened. A folded, yellowed sheet of paper was inside. I gingerly unfolded the page, but I already knew what it was. It was another stolen page from the manuscript.

The usual between-class hustle carried on around me. No one seemed to notice that I held a stolen piece of literary history in my hand.

I snatched a folder from my locker, emptied its contents, and carefully slipped the page inside. I had to find Frank.

I slammed my locker shut and swung my backpack over my shoulder. Clutching the folder to my chest, I moved through the crowd on the way to Frank's locker.

When I reached the end of the hallway, I almost ran right into my brother coming around the corner.

"I found something in my locker," he whispered.

"Does it look something like this?" I asked as I cracked open my folder.

He glanced down at the page. "Oh, yeah."

"Someone is messing with us big-time," I said. "What do we do?"

Frank opened his mouth to answer but stopped when the intercom speakers crackled to life.

"May I have your attention, please," said the principal's voice. "May I have your attention, please."

Everyone in the hallway paused to listen to the announcement.

"The Bayport Police Department is conducting a surprise locker inspection," the principal continued. "Please place your backpacks, purses, or any other bags against the wall and make your way to the gym in an orderly fashion."

My eyes widened. "Oh, man."

CAUGHT ON CAMERA

5

FRANK

JOE AND I TOOK OFF OUR BACKPACKS like everyone else around us. Unlike everyone else, I crouched down and removed a stolen artifact from my bag. Joe stepped closer and opened the folder holding the other page so I could slide mine in on top of his. We joined the slow migration of students toward the gym.

"You think they're looking for the pages?" Joe whispered.

"That's my guess," I replied. The high school had been the subject of surprise locker inspections in the past, but they were very rare. This seemed a little too coincidental.

"I have to ditch this folder," said Joe. "You know they'll take a special interest in us, for sure."

"Hang on," I said. "I'm thinking."

I looked for a place to stash the folder. It needed to be someplace safe, where no one would think to look.

We rounded a corner and were in the main hallway leading toward the gym. Luckily, the sheer volume of students and teachers pouring into the corridor made traffic slow to a crawl.

Then I saw it.

There was a bulletin board up ahead on the right. Tacked-up flyers and announcements covered the rectangular corkboard. Courtney Terrill's petition for more vegan options being served in the cafeteria hung from a large tack at the bottom of the board. Several wrinkled sheets dangled from a black metal clip.

"Hand me the folder," I whispered to Joe. "And cover for me when we get to the bulletin board."

"You got it." Joe slipped me the folder.

I shuffled to the right side of the hallway.

Joe worked on the distraction; he spun around and began walking backward. "Hey! I know whose fault this is!" he shouted. "It was the stink Benny made in chemistry class last week."

As a few of our fellow students laughed, I reached up and unhooked the petition from the tack. I pulled out the manuscript pages and clipped them to the back of the stack of pages as fast as I could.

"I bet the government thinks he came up with a formula to get superpowers," Joe continued. Everyone laughed again.

"You may call me Spider-Benny!" Benny shouted to the crowd.

Once the pages were in place, I hung the petition back amid other Benny nickname ideas and more laughter. "No, Super-Benny!" "Benny the Hulk!" "Bat-Benny!"

I dropped the empty folder, and Joe and I shuffled into the gym. We were surrounded by a discussion about how "Bat-Benny" doesn't make sense, because Batman doesn't have superpowers to begin with, and how the Benny-chemistry scenario is closer to how the Flash got his super speed. Of course, my brother was at the head of this serious philosophical debate.

Inside the gym, Joe and I made our way to one side, trying to find some kind of privacy. The place was so loud with chatter we no longer needed to whisper.

"That was way too close," said Joe. "We really need to figure out who's behind this. Fast."

I nodded. "Yeah, but who would it be?"

"It has to be a student," Joe concluded. "People would notice a stranger slipping stuff into lockers."

"Yeah, and students do that all the time," I agreed. "So no one would care."

"How about the security cameras?" asked Joe. "I bet they recorded whoever did it."

I felt a knot in my stomach. "You mean the same ones that probably recorded us finding the pages and then hiding them?"

Joe's eyes widened. "We have to get to that video before the police think of it."

I followed my brother toward the nearest exit. I wasn't worried about sneaking out of the gym. The place was chaos and filled with milling students. Paper balls and airplanes flew above everyone's heads.

We slipped out the side door behind the bleachers. The door led to the outside of the building, so we ducked as we ran past several classroom windows. I paused to see the police in the hallway beyond an open classroom door. Sure enough, they were going through all the lockers. They had a big job ahead of them, so I guessed that they wouldn't take the time to check behind Courtney's petition.

I caught up with Joe at the end of the building as he peered around the corner. The side entrance was just ahead. He waited a moment longer before motioning me forward. Careful not to draw attention, we turned the corner and walked quickly toward the glass doors. Luckily, the hallway beyond was empty. We opened the doors and snuck inside.

It was just two more turns before we reached the security office. Luck finally seemed to be on our side: the door was unlocked and the room was empty. The school security guard was probably helping the police with the locker search. We snuck in and shut the door behind us.

Joe sat down at the desk in front of the main computer screen. Two smaller screens were on either side. They were each quartered off into eight camera views from around the school. After a few seconds, the screens would switch to a different scene.

"Can you find today's footage?" I asked.

Joe tapped on the keyboard. "I already have, but we have trouble." He pointed to one of the camera views. "That's where we came into the building. This thing recorded us sneaking out and back into the school."

"We're toast," I said.

"Not if I delete the file," Joe suggested.

"That's destroying evidence," I countered.

Joe dug into his pocket. "Okay, 'delete' was not the right word." He pulled out a small USB drive. "I'll move the file to this. After we solve the case, we can turn it over to the police."

"And get busted by Lieutenant Wolfe for meddling," I said.

"Maybe she'll just be happy we found the pages and all will be forgiven," Joe suggested.

I raised an eyebrow. "Really?"

"Or maybe we sneak back in and put the file back," said Joe. "Either way, we don't have time to search the video file right now. We have to take it with us."

I sucked in a deep breath and exhaled. "Okay, do it."

Joe tapped a few more keys. "Okay, first . . . let's stop this thing from recording." He glanced at me over his shoulder. "So we can get out of here without being recorded again." He then plugged in the drive and typed on the keyboard. "Now, moving the file . . . whoa, it's a big one."

A progress bar appeared on the screen as I looked at the changing camera views. The police seemed busy searching lockers and backpacks. Hopefully no one would bother with the security office before the file finished transferring.

"Oh, man," said Joe. "This is going to be awhile."

Only we didn't have awhile. I paced back and forth in the small room to relieve some of the tension.

When I looked back at the screen, the bar was only half complete. Joe was leaning closer to one of the screens.

"What are those two doing?" he asked.

I moved in and saw a police officer and the security officer marching down one of the hallways.

"Where is that?" I asked. "Are they coming here?"

"They sure are," Joe replied.

"We have to get out of here," I said. "Pull the drive."

"I can't," said Joe. "It'll corrupt the file."

"Forget the file," I said. "We can't get caught in here."

Joe leaned closer to the screen. "Just a little longer."

On the surveillance screen, we watched the two men turn a corner and walk down the hallway toward the security room. They were closing in.

I took refuge in the small closet that housed shelves of old computer equipment and cameras. It would be tight, but we could both fit inside.

"Come on," I whispered. "We can hide in here."

Joe looked back and forth from the camera views to the progress bar. It still wasn't finished. "Just a little more."

"Joe," I whispered louder.

The men walked into a view of the hallway outside. They headed straight for the security room door.

"Good enough, I hope," Joe whispered. He jerked the drive out of the computer and dashed toward the closet. He shut the door behind him just as we heard the security office door open.

We held our breath, careful not to make a sound.

"Okay, what do you need?" asked a voice from the other side of the door. It must've been the security officer.

"The lieutenant wants all footage from today," said the police officer.

There was the sound of tapping keys and then, "Uh-oh."

"What's wrong?" asked the police officer.

"The system isn't recording," said the other man. "And there's no file from today. It must not have been recording."

The policeman groaned. "The lieutenant isn't going to be happy. Come on. You better explain it to her."

"Why me?" asked the security officer.

"Because she can't fire you."

We heard the door shut behind them as they left, then waited a few moments before stepping out of the closet.

We both signed with relief.

"Let's get out of here," I said.

"No kidding," agreed Joe.

We took advantage of our location and checked all the camera views before stepping into the hallway. Before long, we had mapped out a clear path back to the gym.

6 ON THE MENU

JOE

WAS AFRAID OF THAT," I SAID AS I EXAMINED the file on my laptop. "When I pulled the USB drive, the file got corrupted."

Frank leaned across the table to look at the screen. "Can you do anything with it?"

"Already on it," I said as I opened one of my recovery apps. I dragged the file into the app, and a progress bar appeared. The bar on the security computer from that morning moved at lightning speed compared to this one. I set it to run in the background and put my laptop away. "It might not work, and it will take a couple of hours."

Frank sighed. "I guess we'll just have to take our chances."

We sat in a booth in our usual after-school hangout spot: the Meet Locker. It was part coffee shop, part diner and basically everyone from Bayport High hung out here after school.

Frank stared out the window. "I'm having second thoughts about where I hid the pages," he said. "What if someone decides to take down Courtney's petition?"

I waved away the suggestion. "You chose the perfect hiding place, bro. That thing has been on the board since the beginning of the school year. The teachers won't take it down because it'll make them look biased. And Courtney hasn't taken it down because it keeps getting more signatures."

"Really?" asked Frank. "People are actually signing it?"

"Oh, yeah," I replied. "Of course some of the names are Taylor Swift, Johnny Depp, and Barack Obama." I smiled. "It's a running gag for some of the guys."

Frank raised an eyebrow. "And how would you know about that?"

I shrugged. "Let's just say I know that Darth Vader flew in from a galaxy far, far away to sign it."

Frank laughed and shook his head.

"Hey, guys!" Chet Morton greeted us as he walked up with two menus under his arm. "Fun day today, huh? I don't know about you, but I got out of an algebra exam." He slid a menu in front of each of us.

I pushed mine away. "How long have you known us? And how long have we been coming here? We always order the same thing."

Chet grinned. "Who knows? You guys might change

your minds today." He glanced at the front of the restaurant. "I'll be back in a minute to take your orders."

I raised a finger. "But we're already ready to—" Chet was gone. I turned back to Frank. "What's up with him?"

Frank was peering over my shoulder toward the front, a grim expression on his face. "Heads-up," he said. "We're about to have company."

Lieutenant Wolfe strolled up to our booth. She did not look happy. "Well, well. Fancy meeting you here."

"Hello, Lieutenant," Frank said. "Can we help you?"

"And by 'help,' he doesn't mean helping with the case," I added. "Just to be clear."

"Is that so?" asked the lieutenant. "Well then, you wouldn't know anything about the anonymous tip we received this morning, would you?"

My brother and I glanced at each other. "Is that what the surprise locker inspection was all about?" asked Frank.

The woman nodded. "Someone claimed the missing manuscript pages were hidden in one of the student lockers."

"Were they?" I asked.

"No, they weren't," she replied. "An entire morning wasted." She placed her hands on her hips. "But I wonder if two amateur detectives who aren't supposed to be detecting tried to help by calling in the tip in the first place."

"I don't know. It sounds as if the tip wasn't so helpful," Frank said. His lips tightened. "If someone really wanted to help, they wouldn't have called in a useless tip."

"Oh, it wasn't completely useless," said the lieutenant. "I did learn something."

"Oh, good," I said, trying to ease the tension. "What was it?"

Lieutenant Wolfe grinned. "Someone spotted you two sneaking out of the gym."

"Not so good," I muttered as I fidgeted with the menu. "Just a harmless bathroom run, that's all."

"Really?" asked the woman. "Brother detectives never pee alone, huh? You won't mind if I search your backpacks, will you?"

I was about to oblige. After all, we didn't have anything to hide. But Frank answered first.

"What's your probable cause this time?" he asked.

I sighed. I knew Frank was irritated with the lieutenant, but this wasn't how you keep a low profile. I thumbed the corner of my menu while they hashed it out.

"Oh, no probable cause," she told him. "But I do have a couple of theories. Since the general public doesn't know about the missing pages, maybe you *did* call in the tip. We'd come up with nothing and you'd make us look foolish . . . again. Maybe you thought I would come to you for help."

Frank shook his head. "Of course not. And your other theory?"

"That you two really did steal the pages. Hector Cruz knows this and he called in the tip. Then you boys snuck the pages out of school somehow. You already think you're above the law—maybe you think you've earned these valuable pages from your favorite author. Maybe Hector sees what I see. He did lose his job because of you guys, after all."

I thought I heard Frank growl.

"I'd give my opinion about your theories, but we're not supposed to be working the case, right?" Frank said through clenched teeth.

The lieutenant shrugged. "Either way, I thought two helpful citizens like yourselves would consent to a simple search."

"Again, I thought we weren't supposed to be . . . helpful," said Frank.

I shook my head. He was really digging in. I thought I might as well look at the menu. Thought perhaps I could turn this day around and try something new. Chet always says a new snack could mean a new direction.

I had no such luck.

I opened the menu to find another missing page covering the sandwich options. Great. It was right there, in front of the police. I quickly shut the menu and tried to act naturally.

"You know, your car is parked two inches over the legal distance from the curb," said the lieutenant. "I was going to let you off with a warning."

"Blackmail now?" asked Frank.

I slid my backpack over and handed it up to Wolfe. "It's cool, bro," I said. "We have nothing to hide, right?"

The police officer took the bag and began digging through it.

Frank rounded on me. "But we're not criminals. They don't have probable cause."

I reached over the table and grabbed my brother's backpack. I locked eyes with him and hoped he'd get with the program. "We give consent, don't we?"

Frank must've seen something in my gaze. It was clear that he didn't like it, but he gave in. "Okay, fine."

The lieutenant searched through each of our backpacks. Of course, there was nothing to find.

"All right, Hardys," said the lieutenant. She handed Frank his backpack. "Don't forget what I said." We watched her walk out of the diner and drive away.

"Why did you give in?" Frank asked. "They had no legal right—"

My brother shut up when I opened my menu, revealing one of the missing pages. His eyes widened and I shut the menu once again.

"Check yours," I instructed.

Frank opened his menu to find another page. "Oh, boy."

I looked around the restaurant. There were a couple of lingering glances left over from Frank's dustup with the police, but no one seemed to be actively watching us.

I turned back to Frank as we both said, "Chet."

Frank slipped the pages from the menus and slid them into his backpack. We grabbed our bags and approached the front counter. Chet was busy wiping it down with a towel. As we got closer, he leaned forward and whispered, "What was up with the cops?"

"Dude, why did you put those in our menus?" I asked.

"And where did you get them?" asked Frank.

Chet chucked. "Come on, it was just a prank. That guy— the friend of yours visiting from out of town? He asked me to do it. Said it would be the perfect joke after what happened with Hector. But he wouldn't tell me what had happened. Will you guys let me in on this now?"

"What guy?" asked Frank, ignoring Chet's question.

Chet cocked his head, clearly confused. "I've never seen him before, but he said he was from out of town so . . . He seemed to know you guys really well." He pointed to the large front windows. "He was standing outside watching while you talked to the police. Oh, no. Did I do something wrong?"

We turned and saw a thin guy wearing a hooded sweatshirt and sunglasses. The hood was pulled down so I couldn't make out his face. When he saw us looking, he climbed onto a bicycle and pedaled down the sidewalk and out of view.

Frank shoved his backpack at Chet, who barely caught it. I did the same. "Watch this for me," he ordered.

"Ditto," I added. "You owe us."

I followed Frank as we ran onto the street.

DÉJÀ VU 7

FRANK

OF COURSE MY BROTHER THE TRACK star pulled out ahead of me as soon as we began the chase. I thought about going back to get my car, but I figured I'd just waste time. Anyway, the guy on the bike pedaled so slowly, it was clear he had no idea we were even chasing after him. I figured we'd catch up in no time.

I was wrong.

Things changed when he glanced back and realized his mistake. He stood as he pedaled, pouring on the speed. He was putting distance between us—and fast.

Joe kept pace at first. My brother knew how to pour on the speed himself. But legs were no match for wheels, and our culprit soon pulled away. I wasn't even in the race when

I saw the bike turn right down Swenson Avenue, though it looked like Joe still had him in his sights.

Taking a risk, I took an immediate right down Juliana Street. If the guy doubled back, maybe we could corner him.

I ran as quickly as I could down the sidewalk. My side began to ache, but I kept going. Luckily, it was after closing time for most of the local businesses; I didn't have to worry about plowing over anyone.

I reached the intersection of Juliana and Winslow Boulevard and skidded to a stop. As I'd hoped, the cyclist had doubled back; now he sped down the sidewalk in my direction. I backed away and hid behind the corner of a building. Maybe the guy hadn't spotted me yet.

I peeked out to see him getting closer. Behind him, Joe had turned the corner and was still in pursuit. A few more feet and I'd leap out to block his path. I hoped I would be enough of a surprise to make him stumble. Maybe even fall off his bike.

Just then, the cyclist cut left and darted into the street. Tires squealed as a car braked, almost slamming into him. The guy wobbled on his bike but kept crossing the road. He disappeared into an alley on the other side.

Joe and I crossed after him, both of us more careful than the rider. We ran behind the stopped car and darted into the alley after him.

I trailed Joe as we sprinted down the narrow alleyway. There was no sign of the cyclist, but we didn't slow down.

Growing up in Bayport, we both knew that this alley was a dead end. If we hurried, we could have the guy cornered.

We slowed when we saw the bicycle lying on the ground. I scanned the area, looking for places where the guy might be hiding. There was nothing but the empty alley ending at a tall wooden fence.

"Think he climbed over?" I asked Joe between heaving breaths.

"He didn't have to. Look." Joe pointed to a broken plank in the fence.

We ran up to it and I pulled half of the wide board away. There was a jagged gap just big enough to squeeze through. Joe carefully shimmied to the other side.

"Come on," he said.

I pushed through the gap and found myself in a very familiar place.

"Déjà vu, huh?" asked Joe as he scanned the construction site.

We'd had a narrow escape here a few years ago when this was little more than a vacant lot. My brother and I had been after a couple of bank robbery suspects. The trail had led us here and the bad guys caught us. We had been tied up and placed in an excavation about to be filled with cement. If we hadn't escaped, Joe and I might've been underneath the slab spread out before us.

It looked as if construction was underway again. Large steel girders jutted out of the slab, and stacks of building supplies and construction equipment filled the area. The site was deserted and silent, so the workers must've gone for the day. A tall chain-link fence sealed off the rest of the area. We hadn't heard the fence rattle, so it was a good bet that the guy hadn't climbed over. He was still here . . . somewhere.

I caught Joe's eye and motioned for him to go left. I would go right. Maybe we could flush out the guy faster if we split up.

We both crept silently through the site. I didn't exactly know what we'd do when we found the mystery man. If we could capture him and turn him in to the police, the pages would be returned. But we'd still get in trouble with the lieutenant for investigating in the first place. Maybe she would go easy on us since this guy was obviously trying to set us up.

None of this made sense, though. Who was this guy and what did he have against us?

An engine roar interrupted my train of thought. It came from Joe's side of the construction site. I looked over to see my brother freeze in front of a tall stack of bricks. He was trying to find the source of the noise too. That's when the bricks begin to move.

"Look out!" I shouted as I sprinted toward Joe.

My brother looked left and right, everywhere but at the stack of bricks behind him. The engine noise echoed around the site, making it hard to pinpoint.

As I neared, the tower of bricks leaned toward him and Joe looked up just as the stack began to loom over his right shoulder. Without thinking, I dove toward my brother and tackled him to the ground; my momentum carried us clear of the falling bricks. We watched as they smashed onto the spot where Joe had just been standing.

"Are you okay?" I asked as we got to our feet.

"Yeah, thanks," Joe replied.

The rumbling died and the sound of footsteps filled the air. The culprit ran through the construction site, back toward the alley. He was halfway through the gap in the fence before Joe and I got up to speed.

"Ah!" the guy shouted as his leg caught on the jagged board.

It barely slowed him down. By the time Joe and I reached the fence, we heard the bicycle speeding off. I peeked through the hole and spotted the suspect turning out of the alley, getting away.

UNINVITED GUEST

8

JOE

WHAT'S THAT WEIRD SMELL?" FRANK
asked as we walked into our house.

"I hope it's not dinner," I replied with
a wince. "Although Aunt Trudy does like
to experiment."

We weren't happy about losing the mystery guy. However,
we both agreed that we were lucky the police hadn't spotted our chase through Bayport. How would we explain that?
Training for my track meet?

We yelled greetings to Aunt Trudy as we climbed the
stairs and went to straight to our rooms. I was anxious to see
if my computer had rebuilt the security footage. I perched
on my bed and pulled my laptop out of my backpack, tapping my foot as the computer powered on.

Now, I'm not the neatest Hardy brother. My desk isn't cleared off and organized like Frank's, but I know where everything is when I need it. I have a very complex "pile" system. I can always tell when something has been added to it.

I was just about to move aside last night's homework papers (placing them onto the correct pile) when I saw an unfamiliar sheet of paper lying on top. Picking it up, I realized that it wasn't so unfamiliar after all: it was another stolen page from the manuscript.

With page in hand, I turned to go show Frank, but my brother stood in the doorway holding up a page of his own.

"Aunt Trudy?" we shouted in unison.

"Yes?" she replied from the kitchen.

Frank and I moved to the head of the stairs. "Did someone stop by today?" Frank asked.

"Yes, dear," she replied as she stepped out of the kitchen and into view.

Frank and I hid the pages behind our backs.

Aunt Trudy wiped her hands on her apron. "The exterminator came by for the yearly treatment."

"That's the smell," whispered Frank.

"Glad it's not dinner," I whispered back.

"Was he ever alone up here?" Frank asked her.

Aunt Trudy shook her head. "Heavens, no. I know better than that." She squinted up at us. "Is anything missing?"

"No," I replied truthfully. "Nothing's missing at all."

Our aunt clapped her hands together. "He did ask me to

pull out everything from under your bathroom sink. I probably didn't get it all back the way it was."

I nodded. "That was it. Thanks, Aunt T."

She turned and waved. "Dinner will be ready soon."

I returned to my room thoroughly creeped out. Frank followed me in and shut the door.

"Dude! He was in our house," I said. "In our rooms."

"I know," agreed Frank. "Not good."

"We *have* to go to the cops now," I said.

"Yeah, but tell them what?" Frank asked.

"Oh, I don't know . . . breaking and entering?" I replied.

"Except that nobody broke in," Frank explained. "Aunt Trudy had an exterminator in and we have stolen goods in our rooms."

"What about Chet?" I asked. "He can vouch for us."

"Yeah, but he's one of our friends," Frank countered. "It'll just look like we're getting our friend to lie for us. This thing with the pages turning up in our possession is just too unbelievable. What if the lieutenant really thinks this would be our way of making them look bad? Or worse, thinks we actually stole the pages?"

"Then what do we do?" I asked. "The guy was in our house."

"We need more evidence." Frank pointed to the laptop. "Maybe we have the guy on video."

"Oh, yeah! I almost forgot." I sat down and opened my laptop—the footage was ready. "Let's see what we have. . . ."

I opened the file and a group of folders appeared. There were twelve camera views to choose from, each with their own video from the day. I played the video from the first folder. It showed a grainy black-and-white view of one of the empty hallways.

"Hey, it worked," I said, leaning closer to the screen. "Where is that?"

Frank studied the screen. "I think that's in front of Mrs. Meehan's art room."

I searched the rest of the folders and found the two that showed our lockers. Frank's locker was closer to the camera on his video file, so I started with that one.

Like the beginning of all the other videos so far, the hallway was empty; school hadn't started yet. I fast-forwarded until students began coming into view, then I slowed the queue a bit but kept the video running at triple speed. A figure zipped by Frank's locker.

"There," Frank said, pointing to the screen.

Rewinding, I got past the point where the figure appeared on-screen and played it at normal speed. The person walked into view and quickly slipped something through the vents in Frank's locker. We recognized her. It was another one of our friends. Amanda Paul.

THE SPIDER'S WEB

9

FRANK

THE NEXT DAY AT SCHOOL, BEFORE we did anything else, Joe and I checked our lockers for any new stolen pages. Luckily, my locker was just as I had left it. Joe's locker was a disaster area, but that was just as he had left it as well. No new pages had mysteriously appeared.

The night before, Joe and I had decided to talk to Amanda at lunch so we could both question her at the same time. We attended our separate classes and tried to act like everything was normal and someone *didn't* have it out for us. Hopefully, Amanda would have some answers.

My morning classes seemed to go on forever. Plus, it was hard to concentrate when my mind kept going back to the case at hand. When the lunch bell finally rang, I got to the cafeteria as fast as I could. Joe was already there, waiting at the main door.

"She get here yet?" I asked.

"Nope." Joe shook his head.

We tried to act casual as students filed past. We didn't want to look like we were waiting to interrogate someone.

"How do you want to play this?" Joe asked. "Start slow, harmless questions? A little small talk? Then maybe go into good Hardy, bad Hardy?"

I rolled my eyes. "I think we just need to find out what she knows."

"Hey, guys," said a voice.

It was Amanda. She'd totally snuck up on us.

"You get those notes yesterday?" she asked.

"What notes?" I asked.

"The envelopes I slipped into your lockers," she replied. "You had to have seen them."

"Uh, yeah, about that . . . ," I said. "We were just looking for you. We wanted to ask you about those."

"Wait," said Joe. "You think you put notes in our lockers?"

Amanda shrugged. "Yeah, what else would they be?"

"Uh, never mind that," I said. "*Why* did you put them in our lockers?"

Amanda looked puzzled. "Eric asked me to. He didn't sign them or anything?"

Eric Watts—another one of our friends.

Joe shook his head. "No, he didn't."

"Wait a minute." She narrowed her eyes at us. "If you didn't know Eric sent the notes, then how did you know *I* put them in your locker?"

Joe and I glanced at each other. "Uh, someone saw you do it," Joe replied.

Yeah, we did, I thought. *On video.*

Amanda raised her hands and laughed. "Okay, whatever the prank was, I'm not involved. Don't shoot the messenger, all right?" She turned and waved to Courtney Terrill, who was walking right toward us.

My heart leaped into my throat. Had Courtney checked the petition? Had she told anyone?

"Hi, Courtney," Joe squeaked as she approached us. "What's up?"

"Hi, guys." Courtney greeted us. "Hey, Amanda. I've been trying to catch up with the Hardy brothers all day. We have important business to discuss."

"Sounds serious. I'll leave you guys to it." Amanda gave us a little wave and joined everyone else filing into the lunchroom.

"So, uh, what's the, uh, business?" I stammered. Yikes, usually we were way more smooth with these types of things. The manuscript pages were making me nervous.

"It's about the crime exhibit at the Bayport Museum." She swung her backpack around and began digging in it. "Hold on a minute."

I took a deep breath. I've learned it's best to wait in these situations. Let the other person reveal their hand before you launch into excuses. Clearly, Joe had learned the same thing. I looked over to see him put his hands in his pockets.

"Got it!" She pulled out a small reporter's notebook and pen. "So, you guys are the teen detectives of Bayport. I'd love to get a quote from you about the exhibit. I'm writing an article for the *Bayport High Gazette*, and I think it would be interesting to get your take on it."

I let out a huge sigh of relief. We were in the clear.

"I'm not sure what to say . . . but it sounds cool!" Joe beamed. "Though, for the record, I'll always be loyal to the dinosaur exhibit. Triceratops forever."

Courtney laughed, "I'm all about the space exhibit myself. What about you Frank, thoughts on the new crime exhibit?"

"Everyone should check out the history of fingerprinting. It's a fascinating story that most people don't know about."

"Great. Thanks, guys!" Courtney put away her notebook. "This article is going to be great. I'm hoping it will good enough to make people realize I'm more than just the vegan girl, you know? That's just one of my passions."

"Totally!" Joe said. "You're also Courtney Terrill, Bayport High's star reporter."

Courtney smiled and went to join her friends in the lunchroom.

Joe and I stared at each other in disbelief.

"That was close," said Joe.

"Yeah," I agreed. "And we still need to go talk to Eric."

We quickly spotted Eric across the lunchroom, sitting at a table with a few of our other friends. Joe was able to drag him away without arousing suspicion. We gathered beside the wall.

"What's up, guys?" Eric asked.

"Amanda said you had her put something in our lockers?" I asked.

Eric's face was blank for a moment. For a second there, I wondered if he was behind the entire thing and he knew he was caught. Then his face lit up.

"Oh, yeah." He smiled. "The letters from your cousin."

"Our cousin?" asked Joe.

"Yeah, the guy said he was visiting from out of town and wanted to surprise you," Eric explained. "He asked me to slip some letters into your lockers. I didn't have time, so I asked Amanda."

"Letters?" I asked.

"Hey, I didn't read them!" Eric laughed.

"What did this guy look like?" I asked.

Eric shrugged. "I don't know . . . tall, thin. Maybe a couple years older than us." He frowned. "How long has it been since you've seen him? You don't remember what your cousin looks like?"

Joe and I shared a look.

Eric's eyes widened. "Oh, snap! You're on a case, aren't you? Was that not really your cousin?"

Joe flinched and glanced around.

I shushed Eric. "Keep it down. The police don't want us working any cases."

Eric put his hands in his pockets. "All right, all right." He glanced around. "I'll keep it on the down low," he whispered. "Just let me know how it turns out, all right?"

"We will, man," said Joe. "And thanks."

Eric returned to his table and Joe and I got in line for lunch. We got our trays and chose an empty end of one of the tables, near the wall.

"All that and nothing to show for it," Joe began. "We still don't know who has it out for us."

"We just know that this guy is using all our friends against us," I added.

"You know what this is?" Joe asked between bites. "This guy is going full Moriarty on us."

It took me a second to catch Joe's meaning. "Oh, yeah. You're right."

Professor Moriarty was Sherlock Holmes's nemesis. Moriarty was a criminal mastermind who mirrored Holmes's intelligence and cunning. He was famous for surrounding himself with a spider's web of minor criminals. That way, if any were caught, their crimes would never lead back to the man in the center of the web, the professor himself. Because of this technique, many characters in the Holmes stories doubted the villain's very existence. In the end it took all of Holmes's detective skills to flush him out and lead to their final battle at Reichenbach Falls.

"So, how do we find out who our Moriarty is?" Joe asked.

"It's someone who knows way too much about us and our friends," I said.

"And someone with a grudge," Joe added. "Obviously."

"You still think it's someone we put away?" I asked.

Joe nodded and took another bite. "Yeah, this person is trying to make us squirm. And clearly has a plan. My only question is who? There's a long list of people that would like revenge."

"We'll go over our notes tonight," I said. "Before that, we have to get those pages back from behind the petition."

"Absolutely," said Joe. "That was way too close."

"I'll grab them after last class," I volunteered. "During the Friday after-school rush."

"Good thinking," said Joe.

Since we'd used up most of our lunch break on the investigation we weren't supposed to be conducting, we had to wolf down our lunch. After that, we went back to class as if everything was normal. But it was everything but normal. I found myself glancing around to see if I was being watched. Would another friend slip us more stolen pages?

When the last bell finally rang, I headed straight for the bulletin board near the main gym entrance. I turned the corner and was relieved to see the stack of papers still hanging from the page clip. I casually set my backpack under the board, unzipped the top, and unhooked the petition.

I had just unclipped the manuscript pages and crouched

down to slip them into my pack when a hand clamped onto my shoulder. I just knew it was Lieutenant Wolfe catching me red-handed.

"I didn't peg you as a vegan, Hardy," said a man's voice.

I slid the pages deeper into my pack as I turned and looked up. It was Coach Smith.

"I'm not, Coach," I said, "I, uh . . ." I fumbled for a pen in my pack. "I just support everyone's right to, uh . . . eat what they want."

"I'm a carnivore myself," said the coach. "My food *eats* their food."

I forced a small chuckle. "Good one, Coach." *Old one,* I thought.

I flipped open the petition and found the last signature. I signed my name at the bottom of the page . . . right under *Harry Potter.*

THE BAYPORT IRREGULARS

10

JOE

'M JUST SAYING," I SAID. "IF THIS GUY IS like Moriarty, and we're like Holmes and Watson, then I'm Sherlock in this scenario."

Frank shook his head and laughed. "No way." He flipped another page in one of his journals. "I'm older. I'd be Sherlock."

I pointed to the stack of journals on his desk. "You keep all the notes on our past cases. Watson wrote stories about their cases. Enough said."

Frank ignored the debate and turned to the next page in the journal. Each page listed out the details of a past case: criminal name, clues, date of arrest. It was the Hardy Archives. "What about the Wilcox brothers?" he asked. "It may not have been a coincidence that we were led to that construction site."

"I thought of that," I said, thinking back to the bank robbers who had tried to make us a permanent part of the building's foundation. "But they went away for a federal crime. There's no way they're getting out of prison anytime soon."

Frank sighed. "Wish we could find out for sure, though."

If an irate crook was targeting us, it wouldn't be the first time. In the past, we had checked in with a couple of contacts in the Bayport PD. The police had access to databases that let them know who was still locked up and who had been released. Unfortunately, we couldn't reach out to any of those contacts without word getting back to Lieutenant Wolfe.

While Frank continued his search, I peeked through the window blinds again. The street looked empty, but I couldn't shake the feeling that we were being watched. So far, the culprit had been in our house and had manipulated our friends. He knew all about us and we knew nothing about him. I had never felt so helpless during a case before.

"There has to be a better way to get a lead on this guy," I said. "What would Holmes do in a case like this?"

Frank closed the journal and got to his feet. "He'd call on his Irregulars."

In the stories, Sherlock would often get help from a group of street kids called the Baker Street Irregulars. They would blend into the background of Victorian London and follow people or keep their eyes and ears open for suspicious activities. They were named after Baker Street, where Holmes and Watson lived—221B Baker Street, to be exact.

"That sounds great and all," I said. "But there isn't a group of homeless kids running around Bayport. And if there was, they certainly wouldn't go unnoticed by the police."

Frank shook his head. "No, but I have an idea for the next best thing." He fished out his phone. "Does Dillon's little brother still run around with that skateboard crew?"

I smiled. "I think so."

After a quick text exchange with our friend Dillon, Frank and I pulled our bikes out of the garage and snuck them through the house. We wheeled them through the backyard and into the alley behind the house. Since the police (and our mystery Moriarty) seemed to be watching for Frank's car, we thought it best to leave from the back on bicycles. Good thing Aunt Trudy was too busy watching her favorite prime-time reality show to notice. We didn't want to explain why we couldn't just ride our bikes out of the garage. Plus, she would have an absolute fit if she spotted us hauling our dirty bikes through her clean house.

We pedaled through the night, carefully sticking to alleys and side streets whenever possible to avoid running across any police patrol routes. It took awhile, but we pulled into the parking lot for the old Save Market grocery store. The place had been closed for several years, and weeds had begun sprouting through the cracks in the pavement. The store itself wasn't our last stop. From what we'd learned from Dillon, our destination was in back.

I followed Frank behind the store and saw, as promised, a

group of young skaters hanging out on the abandoned loading dock. We pulled up just in time to see one of them skate off the lip of the dock. His skateboard spun beneath his feet as he soared through the air. The board righted itself just as the boy neared the ground. He landed on the board's deck flawlessly.

"Nice," I said, impressed with the board flip.

Dillon's little brother, Drew, skated down the side ramp and skidded to a stop beside us. "Hey, guys." He flipped his auburn bangs away from his eyes. "Dillon texted that you were coming by."

"Yeah, we have a strange favor to ask," said Frank. By this time, the other four skaters had gathered around. "We were wondering if you guys could keep your eyes open for a couple of days. Look out for anything suspicious around town."

"We do that already," said one of the skaters. "That's why we find the best places to skate." He exchanged a fist bump with another skater.

"Well, maybe you can hang out in our neighborhood and see if anyone is watching us or our house." Frank gave them our address. "We think someone is pulling some kind of prank on us."

Drew eyed us suspiciously. "Dillon said you guys solve mysteries and stuff. Is this for a case or something?"

"Yes," I told him, figuring it was best to just tell him the truth.

"No," said Frank, glaring at me. "Well, yes and no. But you can't tell anyone about it."

Whoops, guess I was wrong.

"I don't know," one of the other skaters chimed in. "I know that neighborhood. It's pretty boring. No places to pull any tricks."

"We could build a ramp or a grind box," another kid suggested.

Drew held up a silencing hand. "What he means is, how much does this job pay?"

"Pay?" I asked. I hadn't thought of paying them.

"How about a couple of my brother's video games?" Frank asked.

"What?" I asked. He had the answer too handy not to have thought of it beforehand.

The skaters began throwing out the names of popular video games. I had a lot of those games, but I wasn't finished with them and certainly wasn't ready to give them up. My dear brother simply nodded in agreement.

"Borrow," I said, trying to save my games.

"Entire collection," said Drew. "For six months."

"Everything?" I may have squealed.

"Three months," countered Frank.

"Deal," said Drew. He shook my brother's hand.

I stared at Frank in disbelief. "What just happened?"

He patted my shoulder. "Thanks for your sacrifice. I'm sure your homework will be very grateful."

I sighed. I guess I could live without video games for a couple of months. I just wished my brother would've warned me before offering them up as payment.

Frank and Drew exchanged numbers so they could text us with any news. Then we climbed back on our bikes and began the ride home.

"I'm not thrilled with your technique," I said. "But you did it. Now we have our own Bayport Irregulars."

Frank gave a sly smile. "Elementary . . . my dear Watson."

ANOTHER ESCAPE

11

FRANK

THE NEXT MORNING, I CHOSE MY SEAT in the bleachers very carefully. Drew and his friends were watching our house, and we guessed the next place to strike would be at Joe's Saturday track meet. If this crook knew us as well as he seemed to, then he would know about my brother's extracurricular events. I planned to stay extra vigilant while Joe ran with his team. My seat on the end of the bleachers let me keep an eye on both locker room entrances along with my parked car in the distance.

I stayed in the stands so it would appear as if I was just watching the track meet, in case anyone was watching me. And after the past few days, it seemed as if *everyone* was watching me. Not a great feeling. Every passing glance seemed suspect. Every time a classmate greeted me, I expected him or her to pass along another manuscript page. Joe and I have been on a few stakeouts in our day, but I'd never felt like the one under surveillance.

So far, the morning had been uneventful. No one had been near the locker room or my car. I started to think that maybe this wasn't the right play. Maybe the crook wasn't going to strike.

Of course, that's just when I saw him.

At least I thought it might be him. I spotted a custodian moving toward the locker room. He wore a cap and gray overalls and pushed a cleaning cart toward one of the entryways. At first I didn't think anything of it. But then I wondered why a custodian would clean the locker room *before* the meet was over. Wouldn't he wait until after the runners had finished, showered, and cleared out with their gear?

I was already making my way off the bleachers when the mystery worker disappeared through the open doorway.

I made my way down the bleachers and onto the walkway. I resisted the urge to run; I didn't want to draw attention to myself. I had seen a couple of police officers working security, and the last thing I needed was to run into one of them.

As casually as possible, I strolled through the small crowd of spectators, glancing around as I neared the locker room. A custodian might not draw any attention going into the team's locker room, but I might.

I was lucky. I slipped into the open doorway unnoticed.

Once inside, I picked up the pace and jogged down the hallway. I almost immediately slammed into the cleaning cart. It had been abandoned in the middle of the short hallway. Now I knew this guy was an imposter.

I squeezed by the cart and eased toward the main locker room. The guy definitely didn't know anyone was following him; the sounds of locker doors slamming shut and gym bags falling could be heard down the hallway. Still, I kept my back to the wall as I reached the doorway and carefully peered inside. The custodian's back was to me as he searched the lockers. At worst, this was a real custodian looking to raid the athletes' valuables while they were on the field. At best, this was our guy, searching for Joe's locker to plant a manuscript page there. Either way, he didn't belong there. I just needed to see his face.

"Hey!" I shouted.

Okay, not my best plan. He didn't even turn to look. He knew he was busted and took off sprinting into the shower room.

I ran after him, but he was through the opposite side of the building by the time I got to the showers. The double doors on the other side of the room swung shut as I entered.

I made a break for the doors. Unfortunately, they didn't open and I just ran into them.

I caught my balance and pushed them again. The heavy wooden doors gave a little but didn't budge. The custodian—or whoever he was—must have barred them with something on the other side. That's when I remembered the other doors that opened onto another short hallway, leading to the other locker room entrance. I spun around and ran back the way I had come. I slipped past the cart again and ran outside. Slowing my pace so I wouldn't draw any attention, I made my way around the building. From where I had been sitting all morning, I knew that this second entrance, the one closest to the field, was in full view of the spectators. I couldn't look like I was the one who was up to no good.

Trying to act as nonchalant as I could, I walked toward the other entryway. I rounded the corner and hoped to run into the crook coming the other way.

The hallway was empty.

Undeterred, I stepped inside and saw why the doors to the showers had been impassible. A field hockey stick was jammed through both door handles. There was also a pile of clothes on the floor. I knelt and picked up a pair of gray overalls and a baseball cap. The crook had slipped out of them and out of the building before I got there without ever showing his face. Now he would be able to blend in with the rest of the spectators. In other words, he had gotten away. Again.

12

BACK TO WORK

JOE

"OKAY, THIS IS GETTING TO BE RIDICU-lous," I said after Frank finished telling me what happened during my track meet. We sat in his car, watching everyone else leave the event. "I'm not blaming you for losing the guy," I went on. "I'm just sick of waiting for this guy to make the next move."

"Yeah, me too," Frank agreed. "Another wasted day with nothing to show for it."

I pointed to the two medals hanging around my neck. "What about these?" I had won second place in the hundred-yard dash, and our team had come in first during one of the relays. We were going to regionals.

Frank smiled. "You know what I mean."

"Anything from the Irregulars?" I asked.

Frank may have lost sight of the bad guy, but he'd been able to check in with Drew and his fellow skaters.

"All quiet back home," Frank replied.

"You know, having the Irregulars was a great idea and all," I said. "But maybe we're going about this the wrong way."

"What do you mean?" asked Frank.

"Instead of asking ourselves what Sherlock Holmes would do," I explained, "maybe we should be asking what the Hardy brothers would do."

"We're doing it," said Frank.

"No, we're not." I shook my head. "What if this was happening to someone else? What if someone else was being taunted like this?"

Frank's eyes lit up. "We would try to solve the original case."

It was true. Since that first night, Frank and I had been so preoccupied with being framed that we had only recently tried to figure out who would target us in the first place. We were all defense and no offense.

"We still have Lieutenant Wolfe to worry about," Frank pointed out.

"True," I agreed. "But if we end up being 'detained'"—I made air quotes as I said the word—"then at least it'll be after my track meet."

"And we could fill the police in on what we've learned so far," added Frank.

"Say, what *about* the lieutenant?" I asked. "Do you think she could be setting us up?"

Frank thought for a moment. "How so?"

"She could warn us not to investigate and then get someone to plant the pages so we have no choice but to investigate," I explained. "Busting us might make her look good to the chief when he gets back."

"That's a good motive," said Frank. "But that's still playing defensive. Let's put that on the back burner for now and figure out how the pages were stolen in the first place."

I pulled out my phone. "I know someone who can help with that."

I shot a text to Hector and had him meet us at the Meet Locker. Fifteen minutes later and we were all at our favorite booth in the back.

"Hey, guys," Hector said as he sat down. "What's up?"

"We'd like you to tell us more about the manuscript," Frank said.

Hector glanced around. "I told you that I'm supposed to call that lieutenant if you start asking questions about the case."

Frank leaned in. "Are you going to?"

Hector raised an eyebrow. "Do I need to?"

"No," Frank replied. "At least not yet. Not until we figure this thing out." He glanced over at me. "Then I think we'll have to tell her what happened."

I leaned back. "And get some time off from school while we're locked up for investigating a case."

"No kidding?" asked Hector. "She said that?"

Frank nodded. "In so many words."

"Okay," said Hector. "What do you want to know?"

"When did the manuscript arrive?" asked Frank.

"Was it in a crate or a regular box?" I added.

"Who had access to the manuscript once it arrived?" Frank pushed.

Hector held up a hand. "Whoa, slow down. Slow down."

"Sorry," I said. I think Frank and I were a little excited to be back doing what we do best—getting to the heart of the mystery. I had to admit, it felt good to be on the offensive for a change.

"The manuscript arrived last Monday," Hector explained. "I was there when Josh signed for it. It came through a special courier in a small wooden crate."

"Was the crate sealed?" Frank asked.

"Yeah," replied Hector. "I watched Josh open it. The crate was filled with foam packing peanuts, and the manuscript was wrapped tight in bubble wrap."

"Who else had access to it before we saw it?" I asked.

Hector thought for a moment. "Just Josh, I think." He shrugged. "And me, I guess."

"Are you sure?" asked Frank.

"Pretty sure," Hector replied. "After Josh unwrapped it, he put on some white gloves and took it into his office. He wanted to read it. Like he said that night, he's a big Sherlock Holmes fan."

Frank and I looked at each other.

"The next time I saw the manuscript, it was on display like you saw," Hector finished. "I didn't see anyone touch it again until you guys. A bunch of people work at the museum, though."

"That's great, man," Frank said. "I think you helped a lot."

Hector smiled. "You think so? If you find out who stole the pages, maybe I can get my job back."

"Yeah, about that," I said. "The other day you told me you 'stumbled on' your new job. How did that happen anyway?"

"Oh, yeah. That was weird," he replied. "I came out of a store and found a flyer on my car. It said how they were hiring at the museum. When I got there, I thought I'd have to wait in line, you know? I mean if they're putting flyers on everyone's cars, they must be desperate. But I was the only one there. Josh just about hired me on the spot."

"That didn't seem strange to you?" asked Frank.

"Hey, I was just happy for the job," Hector replied. "It was an easy one too. And fun—Josh is a great guy." He jutted a thumb over his shoulder. "They're not hiring here, unless Chet messes up and gets fired."

"Hey, why do you like Josh so much?" I asked.

"He was super fun to talk to. He loved hearing about all our friends from school and all the pranks we've pulled."

I looked at Frank. We had gotten what we needed.

"Thanks, Hector. I'm really sorry about your job. But I

have a feeling those pages are going to turn up sooner rather than later."

Frank and I said our goodbyes and practically skipped back to his car. Things were looking up.

"You thinking what I'm thinking?" I asked my brother.

Frank nodded. "I think it's time to return the pages to the museum."

CONFRONTATION 13

FRANK

I DROVE BACK TO OUR HOUSE TO RETRIEVE the pages. As we turned down our street, we spotted Drew and his friends pulling tricks on their homemade grind box. One of the skaters hopped up and slid his board down the corner of the long rectangular box.

"Hey, when this is over, we should give that thing a try," Joe suggested.

I smirked. "Ah, how quickly we forget the skate park incident."

Joe rubbed his left forearm. "It was just a hairline fracture."

We pulled into the driveway and Joe ran inside to get the pages. Soon he was back in the car with another inconspicuous school folder. I backed out of the driveway and we headed for the museum.

We arrived just before closing, so the parking lot was mostly empty. Of course, this time we entered through the front door.

We made our way to the special exhibit hall and spotted Josh Jenkins. He was speaking with a young couple in front of the fingerprinting exhibit. We hung back until we caught his eye. Jenkins excused himself and strolled over to us.

"The Hardy brothers, right?" he asked. "Frank and Joe?"

Joe held out his hand. "That's right. Good to see you again."

Josh shook his hand. A friendly smile lit up his face. "Hector told me about some of the cases you've solved. I half expected you to show up before now and ask about the theft."

"Well, Mr. Jenkins, we do want to ask you a few questions," I said.

"Please, call me Josh," he said. "But I have to warn you. I was instructed by the police to let them know if you came around."

"Well, we do have some questions," Joe said. "I guess it'll be up to you if you want to call the police or not afterward."

"Is there somewhere we can talk in private?" I asked.

"Sure," Josh agreed. "In my office."

We followed him through a door on the back wall. It led to a small hallway full of employee offices. Josh led us into his and shut the door. He took his seat behind his desk.

"Okay, shoot," he said.

"Well, let's start with this," I said as I placed the folder onto his desk.

Josh opened the folder and scanned the contents. "Well, look at that. The missing pages."

"That's seven of them. So there are three more still missing," Joe explained.

"And you don't seem very surprised," I added.

Josh closed the folder. "Why should I be? The police suspected you from the beginning. You snuck in here after hours, after all. I'm not sure why you'd return them now, though."

"Someone has been planting those on us," said Joe, "and then trying to get the police to catch us red-handed."

Josh reached for his telephone. "That sounds like a story to tell the police."

I reached out a hand. "Before you call, let me ask another question. Where were you this morning?"

Josh paused. "Why do you ask?"

"Because someone tried to plant another page in my brother's things during the track meet," I replied.

"And I have a question too," Joe added. "Where were you Thursday morning, before eight a.m.?"

"I was here," Josh replied. "I work here."

"Are you sure you were here?" I asked. "Because someone had our friends deliver those pages to us. Someone who was young enough to convince our friends that he was our cousin, or just another friend they've yet to meet."

"I'm twenty-eight," said Josh.

"Yeah, but you look younger," said Joe.

"Thanks for the compliment," said Josh. He picked up the phone. "But you said I could call the cops after your questions, so I'm calling them. You can tell them your outlandish story."

"Do you really want to do that?" I asked. "Because the guy we chased the other night hurt his right leg on a jagged piece of wood."

Josh froze. The friendly smile had dropped from his face.

"I'm sure the police would be interested to know about any wounds on your leg," I continued.

Josh slowly put the phone back. He stared at us for a moment before dropping his gaze with a sigh. "Okay. It . . . it was me."

"Why?" I asked. I was stunned. Any halfway decent criminal could've come up with something to explain the leg. Better keep this guy talking. "What did we ever do to you?"

Josh shook his head. "You didn't do anything to me." He stood and put his hands in his front pockets. "I don't know why he targeted you."

"He?" asked Joe. "So you're not the Moriarty here?"

"Moriarty?" asked Josh. Then a wave of recognition washed over his face. "Oh, I can see why you'd think that." He plopped back into his chair. "No, I'm not behind this. Awhile back, I received a call. It was a man's voice. He knew everything about me. Things I have tried very hard to keep secret. I made some mistakes when I was a kid—I hung out with the wrong crowd and was involved in some thefts. Art thefts. When we were caught, I was able to make a deal with the police and keep it all off my record. I turned things around and got this job. My dream job. But if my employers knew about my past, they wouldn't allow me to stay. An art thief managing a museum? Not likely. The man threatened to expose me. He knew all about you, too, about your old cases. He orchestrated this entire thing. I had no choice. I'm sorry."

"He set up everything?" I asked.

"Everything," replied Josh. "He had me order the manu-script, hire Hector, befriend him and learn about you and your other friends, plant the seed in him about inviting you to the museum." He covered his face with his hands. "Oh, I had to cut the pages from the manuscript. I was as careful as possible. I wasn't lying before. I'm a huge fan. It killed me to fold the pages, to put a crease in them."

"Okay. *Now* you can call the police," Joe suggested.

Josh's eyes widened. "Now that you know about him, we can't. He forbade it. Whoever this is, he's not done until you two get locked up."

THE IRREGULARS

DELIVER

14

JOE

I **CAN'T BELIEVE WE'RE GOING TO LET HIM GET** away with it," I said as Frank drove us home. "That guy made our lives miserable the past few days."

"It's not his fault," Frank said. "You heard him. The guy's just trying to protect the life he created. Now we have to find the real crook for all three of us."

I had really thought he would be it. All the evidence pointed to Jenkins. If we hadn't been so worried about the lieutenant's warning, we would've figured it out sooner. Now we were back where we started. We thought we had uncovered our own personal Moriarty, but Jenkins had just been another pawn. We should've known it wouldn't be that easy.

Frank gave Jenkins our phone numbers. If the guy heard from the mastermind of our misery, he was supposed to let us know. But could we trust him? And would he trust us to discover the man's identity so the police could finally get involved? There were too many ifs in the plan for me to feel comfortable.

We turned onto our dark street and didn't see any sign of the skaters. I suppose even Bayport Irregulars had to eat dinner sometime. We pulled into the driveway and climbed out of the car. As soon as the car doors shut behind us, Frank's phone chimed with a text alert.

"It's Drew," Frank told me. "He wants us to meet him at the side of the house."

"That's strange—why wouldn't he just come in?"

Frank just shrugged in reply, and without another word, we slipped around the corner.

"Sup?" said Drew from the shadows. "I didn't know if that guy would cruise down the street again."

"What guy?" I asked.

Drew held out a folded sheet of paper. "The guy who gave me this."

Frank took the paper and opened it. I had an idea what it was before I saw the writing on the page.

"It's another page," said Frank. "What did he want you to do with it?"

"He wanted me to put it into your car when you got back. He even told me your back door was broken and would be unlocked," Drew replied.

Frank just shook his head.

"What did he look like?" I asked.

Drew shrugged. "I don't know. It was dark and he never got out of his car."

"You know, you probably shouldn't be taking things from strangers in cars," Frank said.

"I wouldn't normally," said Drew. "But the rest of my crew was there, and you told us to keep an eye out for anything strange."

"He's got a point," I told my brother.

"Besides, he gave us fifty bucks," Drew added.

"Fifty bucks?" I asked. "For planting the page in my car?"

"No," Drew replied. "For busting out one of your taillights."

"Whoa," I said.

"Did you get a license plate number?" Frank asked.

"No, his plates were removed," Drew replied. "But a couple of the guys followed his SUV. We know where he went."

"Got an address?" I asked.

Drew shook his head. "Be better to show you. It's a weird garage downtown. I can get the crew back here in a couple of hours and take you there."

"That's great," said Frank. "Meet us in the alley behind our house."

"What about the fifty bucks?" asked Drew. "Can we keep it?"

Frank shrugged. "I don't see why not. Pretty sure you're going to earn it."

Drew narrowed his eyes. "What do you mean?"

"Well, I think you're going to bust out one of my taillights like you promised," replied Frank.

"Really?" I asked my brother.

"Josh said that this guy wouldn't stop until we were locked up, right?" Frank had that gleam in his eye I didn't like. "I have a plan. Actually, I have two plans." He turned back to Drew. "Wait until I text you and be sure to get the left one. It's cracked already because *somebody* borrowed my car and backed into a signpost."

"Oh, yeah," I said, rubbing the back of my neck. "I was supposed to fix that, too."

Frank smiled. "Well, now you'll really have to."

HARDYS' GREATEST HITS

15

FRANK

AFTER DINNER WITH AUNT TRUDY, Joe and I went upstairs and dug out our old skateboards, grabbed a couple of knit hats and flashlights, and snuck out back. The hats weren't us trying to dress the part. We certainly didn't want to look like two lame older kids trying to imitate the young skaters. But we did want to somewhat hide our identities from the odd glance in our direction.

Involving the police was inevitable. I had explained my plan to Joe and how the police played a big part. If we found the bad guy in his hideout, we would call them immediately. If not, it was on to plan B and the police would be involved anyway. Maybe we'd solve the case. Maybe we'd get locked up ourselves like the lieutenant promised. One way or another, this was going to end tonight.

Drew and his friends were waiting for us in the alley. Joe and I put our boards down and joined the skaters as we rolled into the night.

As far as disguises go, this was pretty good. No one would be able to tell the Hardys were part of the pack of skaters zipping through town. Of course, we were the only two skaters who didn't ollie onto every sidewalk and pull grinds on passing curbs.

We rode the sidewalk down Oak and turned right onto Daley. I almost wiped out on the quick turn. It had been way too long since I had skated.

As our group rolled down Daley, a police cruiser coasted toward us. Joe and I both turned away as we passed the patrol car. I watched its reflection in the shop windows. The car slowed and put on its turn signal. It was going to turn around and investigate the group of skaters rolling through the night.

Drew must've sensed the same thing. "Hardys, follow me!" he shouted. "Everyone else, go straight and let the cops catch up to you."

"Hassled by the man again," mocked one of the other skaters. The rest laughed.

Drew zipped down a side street to the right. Joe and I followed as best we could. Luckily, we were around the corner before the squad car's headlights swung around and lit the sidewalk.

Hopefully the patrolling officers hadn't gotten an accurate head count as they passed us the first time and wouldn't notice that three skaters were missing when they caught up with the group. I glanced back and saw the police car roll past, following the others. We were good.

Joe and I followed Drew down a few more side streets and back alleys. He kept us off the main roads, probably to avoid any more near misses with the police.

We turned down Washington and headed into the older, industrial part of Bayport. The traffic thinned to nothing as we passed closed warehouses and old factories.

Drew rolled to a stop and pointed. "Up there. The one with the blue door, next to that streetlight. We used to raid their Dumpster for building supplies."

"We'll take it from here," I said. "Thanks."

Drew spun his board around and prepared to kick off. "I'll wait for your text?"

I nodded. "Thanks, Drew."

After Drew skated away, Joe and I picked up our boards and walked down the sidewalk.

"You recognize this place, right?" Joe asked.

"I was going to ask you the same question," I replied.

This was yet another location from one of our past cases. A couple of years ago, our friend's new car was stolen. We eventually uncovered a ring of car thieves who used this very garage to repaint the cars in order to smuggle them out of town. My brother and I were trapped in a painting tent and were nearly overcome by the fumes.

"Do you think one of those guys is behind all this?" Joe asked as we stepped closer.

"Did they seem like the type to create such a complicated plan to frame us?" I asked back.

"Not really," Joe admitted.

"Whoever it is, hopefully we can catch him here and call the police," I whispered.

We moved in and crept up to the small window beside the closed bay door and peeked inside. The nearby streetlight shone in through the window. We couldn't make out everything inside, but we could see that the place was empty. Whoever the skaters followed here was long gone.

Joe moved to the oversize garage door and knelt. "Think the lock is still busted on this thing?"

I joined him. "Only one way to find out."

We both grabbed the bottom of the door and lifted. The door moved but very slowly and only with all the power we could muster. After it was a couple of feet off the ground, we stopped. The door remained in place. Joe and I crawled under, pulling our skateboards in after us.

We both switched on our flashlights and examined the inside. It was just as I remembered it, except without all the paint equipment. The area was mostly open, with a small office alcove beside the only window.

I shined my flashlight beam up at the ceiling. "That's why the door was so hard to open." A garage door opener had been installed since the last time we had been there. I followed a connecting conduit to a switch on the wall. I hit the switch and the door rolled shut.

"Check it out," Joe said, examining the floor. His flashlight lit on two fresh-looking gouges on the cement floor. They were about four feet apart, and each was shaped like a small right angle. "What were they doing here?"

I was more interested in the tire tracks leading into the garage. Two parallel red tracks started at the door and crossed the bay.

Sherlock Holmes collected soil samples from all over London. He could compare mud from someone's shoe to one of his specimens and deduce where in London that person had been. This was all well and good for Victorian England, where the closest thing to pavement was a cobblestone street. No use collecting soil from all over Bayport, since most of our streets were paved. But there was only one place nearby with a red clay road.

Finally. A real clue.

"What does that remind you of?" I asked Joe.

Joe leaned in for a closer look. "The road leading to the city dam." He looked at me in disbelief. "Is this guy playing tracks from our greatest hits album, or what?"

My brother and I had had another case end on the dam itself. And let's just say that it didn't end well. If our Moriarty knew about the sites of our many near-death experiences, then the city dam ranked up there with the best of them. Now we had a clue leading us to the next site in question. Maybe we could finally get ahead of the guy.

"Come on," I said. "Let's get out of here." I headed toward the garage door. "It's time to put plan B into action."

"Like Jenkins said, this guy won't stop until we're locked up," said Joe. "So one of us needs to get locked up."

I sent Drew a text.

PLAN B 16

JOE

I SAT ON MY BIKE AT THE TOP OF THE HILL OVER-looking our street. I had taken the alley to make sure no one could see me get into position and parked in the shadows. I could see almost the entire street laid out before me; it didn't take long before the headlights of Frank's car lit our house. I watched the car back out of the driveway, the white bulb behind the broken taillight shone almost as brightly as the reverse lights.

I kept my lookout as the car slowly pulled away. As we hoped, one of the parked cars pulled out; the brown SUV's headlights turned on, and it began to follow my brother's car. I pushed off and followed both of them.

Frank's car was cruising slowly enough that I had no trouble keeping up with the car following far behind. Like the most boring parade in the world, we snaked through neighborhood streets on our way toward the main part of town.

Then Frank's car came to a complete stop at a four-way intersection and took a right. A police cruiser followed him through, snapping on its blue and red flashing lights. We were right on schedule.

I slowed and stopped as the SUV pulled over to the curb and turned off its headlights. My brother's car pulled over in the distance.

The cop car stopped behind my brother's and two officers got out. They walked up on each side of Frank's car, their flashlight beams washing over the car as they went. While one officer stood at the driver's window, the other inspected the backseat with his flashlight. He leaned closer to the car before opening the back door. The officer reached in and came out with a sheet of paper. He held it and examined it with his flashlight. Of course I couldn't make out the words from this distance, but I already knew what it was. It was the stolen manuscript page that Drew had planted on my brother's backseat. The driver was caught red-handed.

Fortunately, the SUV pulled away from the curb and rolled forward. It must have been satisfied with the traffic stop. I prepared to follow on my bike. Unfortunately, the car began a U-turn.

I pedaled hard and headed for the space between two parked cars. I skidded to a stop and climbed off my bike just as the SUV completed its turn. I ducked down when its headlights snapped on and it drove in my direction.

Once the car passed, I climbed back onto my bike and pedaled after it. No longer trailing my brother's car, the SUV drove much faster. I had to work to keep up with it. Luckily, it couldn't pick up much speed driving through the short residential streets.

I kept pace as the SUV zigzagged through the different neighborhoods. But when it turned onto one of the main roads leading out of town, I knew that there was no way I'd be able to keep up. I turned onto the road after it and shifted my bike up to its highest gear. I pedaled as fast as I could and was up to a decent speed. The car's taillights grew smaller and smaller ahead of me.

But I had a pretty good idea where it was going. This is my hometown, after all.

ANOTHER FAMILIAR PLACE

17

FRANK

THE PAVEMENT TURNED TO RED GRAVEL beneath my bicycle tires and my handlebars wobbled when I turned onto the uneven terrain of the dam's small access road. The roar of the dam's spillway grew louder the closer I got.

I hoped Hector made out okay with the police. Plan B was to give the crook exactly what he wanted. We had hoped to make him think that Joe or I had been stopped by the police for the broken taillight. Then, when the cops found the stolen manuscript page, they would arrest one of us. Little did he know, we'd asked Hector to drive Frank's car. Our friend was sure to be brought in for questioning, but instead of confessing to a crime, he would tell them everything that had been happening, as we had explained it to him.

For better or for worse, Lieutenant Wolfe would find out we had been investigating the crime. I just hoped we could give her a crook to go with that crime. Maybe that would lighten the punishment.

The clay tire tracks were our last and only lead to go on.

I saw the gravel road stretch up a hill before me in the moonlight. I switched to a lower gear and pumped harder as I drove up the incline. The ground leveled off when I reached the edge of the dam itself. The small metal gate meant to keep vehicles off the dam was wide open. I seemed to be on the right track.

I pedaled onto the dam and pulled to a stop to catch my breath. The deafening sound of rushing water masked my heavy breathing. I peered over the side and saw giant white streams of water blasting from openings in the side of the tall dam. The water spread as it dropped hundreds of feet to the river below. Through the mist, I saw the small river snake away into the woods beyond.

The last time I was here, I almost fell over the side myself. My brother and I were on the trail of an art thief named Bill Reynolds. We had tracked him to the dam and found his stash of stolen art in the pump house in the middle of the dam. After a confrontation where Reynolds tried to push me over the side, the art thief had gone over himself. The man had survived the fall and had been sent to prison. But this was yet another location where the Hardy brothers had nearly met their end.

I got back onto my bike and pedaled across the dam. The surface was cement and level so I made better time. I hid my bike behind the old pump house. The building wasn't much more than a small shed that had fallen into disrepair. The dam had since been automated, and the building seemed to be abandoned to all but the occasional vandal. Graffiti decorated the walls, and most of the small windows had been smashed. The main door was held shut with a small padlock.

I pulled out my flashlight and examined the lock. It was new and oddly low on the door, as if it had been installed by a kid. I moved to the window and shined the beam through the broken glass. The room was empty, the equipment having been removed long ago. Only a few old worktables and empty pallets remained.

The last time I was here, Reynolds had worked at the station and had stashed his stolen art behind large banks of equipment. Now there didn't seem to be anywhere to hide anything. Still, the lock on the door suggested something was inside. I rolled my bike to the side of the building and found a window with the least amount of jagged glass. I used a piece of wood to knock away the remaining shards before carefully climbing through.

Once inside, I took a closer look at the interior of the shed. More graffiti tags decorated the walls, while empty spray paint cans and trash littered the floor. It seemed to be a strange collection to be kept under lock and key. Maybe the city had installed the lock to keep more kids from coming up here. Maybe some kids just wanted to lock up their fun new clubhouse.

My flashlight's beam fell onto an old worktable. A blue folder sat on its dusty surface. I crept closer and opened the folder and found two pages from the manuscript. The clues had paid off; I was definitely in the right place.

I saw something out of the corner of my eye and killed the flashlight. Two white dots appeared at the other side of the dam. They were headlights. Someone was coming.

I glanced around for a place to hide. The last time we were here, there had been plenty of things to duck behind. Now there was nothing but shadows.

The car was approaching fast. I couldn't hear the engine over the sound of the rushing water, but the lights grew brighter. They streamed through the pump-house windows, chasing away what shadows remained. I crouched down against the wall. It was too late to crawl back out the way I had come.

I crept toward the door as the car pulled to a stop in front of the building. The headlights switched off and the interior was filled with deep shadows once more. I couldn't hear the car door open over the sound of the water, but I heard the rattle of the padlock.

The only choice I had was to hug the wall beside the door and wait for the crook to enter. Then I could sneak out through the open door. Hopefully the sound of the water would mask my footsteps. Once outside, I could call the police and we would have our Moriarty.

The door opened and a tall figure marched in. He headed straight toward the worktable. I didn't stick around to find out who he was. I ducked outside and pulled out my phone. I dialed 911, but the call failed.

I groaned inwardly. Why is there never cell service when you need it most?

"Hey!" a voice shouted.

Caught, I spun around and was blinded by a flashlight. I squinted but could only make out a silhouette at first. He lowered the light and my eyes slowly adjusted to the dim moonlight. That's when I recognized him.

Josh Jenkins held the flashlight in one hand and a pistol in the other.

LAST RELAY 18

JOE

NEVER REALIZED JUST HOW HARD IT WAS TO
pedal a bike at full speed *and* make a phone call. I
gripped my wobbling handlebar with one hand and
redialed my brother for the third time. Once again, the
call just went to voice mail. I hung up and glanced at
the screen. I suddenly knew why my calls weren't getting
through. The closer I got to the dam, the weaker my cell
signal became.

I shoved my phone back into my pocket and concentrated
on getting to the dam as quickly as possible. The turnoff
was only another mile away, but my strength was dwindling.
With the track meet, the skateboard ride, and the bike ride
across town, I was nearly spent.

I made it a few more yards before something snapped

below. My legs pedaled faster with no resistance whatsoever. My bicycle chain had broken.

Then the dangling chain tangled around my back tire and I lost control. I swerved off the road and couldn't keep my balance when the tires hit the soft shoulder. My bike and I tumbled to the ground.

Breathing hard, I got to my feet. I only had a couple of scrapes and bruises after my tumble, but my bike wasn't so lucky. The front tire was warped and the broken chain was tangled around the spokes of the back tire. I wasn't getting to the dam on that tonight.

I left the bike where it was and began to run down the road. I couldn't let Frank handle Bayport's Moriarty alone. I kept telling myself it was just like one of my long-distance relays.

As I neared the red mud turnoff, the trees around me began to brighten. I glanced back and spotted headlights approaching. I paused and waved from the grassy shoulder but kept running. Maybe I could get a ride. The night grew brighter as the vehicle approached. It was a big white van. It slowed and pulled up alongside of me.

The passenger window lowered. "You okay, son?" asked the man driving.

I stopped and leaned forward to catch my breath. I held up a finger, letting him know that I wasn't ignoring the question. "Bike . . . trouble," I said between breaths.

I glanced up and got a better look inside. A heavyset man

sat behind the wheel. He had thick white hair and a white beard. He wore a friendly smile, and he was clearly concerned about the kid running alone in the dark.

"Can I give you a ride or something?" the man asked.

I held up another finger as I caught a few more breaths. Not getting into cars with strangers may have been Safety 101—it's the first thing they taught us in elementary school, after all—but this was an emergency. I didn't know what kind of situation my brother was in, and going by our track record, it could be a matter of life and death.

"Thanks," I said. I was breathing easier now. "That would be great."

I heard the door locks *click* and I opened the passenger door. I climbed in and buckled up.

"Where you headed?" the man asked.

I pointed ahead. "Do you know where the city dam is?" I asked. "Down a little dirt road, up on the right?"

"Sure do," he said as he put the van in gear. "Been there many times."

The man began to drive, and I noticed how the van had been modified. Instead of pedals, the man accelerated using a small lever on the steering wheel. Another lever jutted out and must've been the brake.

I glanced over my shoulder and saw that the rest of the van was open; no other car seats were installed. However, a wheelchair was parked just behind the two front seats. There was some kind of lift installed just behind it, connected to a large door on the passenger side. It must have been how the man exited the vehicle in his wheelchair.

"Thanks again," I said, finally catching my breath. "This is kind of an emergency."

"You in some kind of trouble?" the man asked.

"No," I replied. "But I have a feeling my brother is."

COMING TOGETHER

19

FRANK

BOY, WAS I IN TROUBLE.

I don't know what kind of fear our Moriarty put into Josh Jenkins, but it was enough for him to get a gun involved and aim it right at my chest.

I slowly raised my hands. "Look, Josh, we can figure this out. I know this guy threatened your family, but we can go to the police."

Jenkins shook his head. "No police. I told you that already."

"Okay, okay," I said. "No police. But my brother and I can help you. We can find out who—"

Josh sneered. "Oh, yeah. Bayport's big detectives. Following all the clues. Well, guess what? Your brother's in

103

jail, Josh Jenkins is going to disappear, and you're going for a little swim."

"Disappear?" I asked. "What are you talking about?"

He flicked the pistol twice, motioning me toward the edge of the dam. "Come on, get over there."

From the corner of my eye, I spotted headlights in the distance. Someone was driving onto the dam. Josh hadn't noticed them yet. I moved toward the edge as he instructed. But I inched away from the approaching headlights, making Josh turn his back to them. I didn't know who was coming, but between keeping an eye on me and the sound of the water, maybe Josh wouldn't notice right away. I might get a chance to run for it.

"Let's go," Josh ordered. "Climb over."

I backed against the handrail. It came up to my waist, and it wouldn't be any trouble to swing my legs over. But past the rail was a drop into the spillway that I didn't think I'd survive. I wasn't in a big hurry to climb over to find out. I had to stall for time.

"There has to be another way," I said. "Maybe there's something else. . . ."

"Something more important than family?" asked Josh.

Behind him, the headlights grew brighter and caught Josh's attention. I thought this would be my chance to get away. However, Josh backed toward the pump station, letting him cover both me and the approaching vehicle.

A white van I didn't recognize pulled to a stop behind

Josh's SUV. The passenger door opened and Joe stepped out.

"Stay in the car, sir," Joe told the driver. He raised his hands and slowly walked toward us. "Mr. Jenkins? Josh? What's going on?"

"Well, look who it is," said Josh. "I thought you'd be rotting in a cell about now. How did you talk your way out of that one?"

While Joe approached, I noticed the driver of the van moving around inside. Was he going to try something?

"Listen, Josh," Joe continued. "We can work this out. No one has to get hurt."

Jenkins shook his head. "Stop calling me that. I'm sick of going by that name."

Behind Joe, a wide door slid open in the side of the van. A bearded man in a wheelchair appeared and jutted out on a special lift. The lift slowly lowered to the ground.

"Then what's your name?" Joe asked.

"Bill Reynolds," Jenkins replied.

Joe and I exchanged a glance. "No way," said Joe. "That guy was in his forties. You're way too young."

The van's lift reached the ground with a loud *crunch*. Its corners chipped away bits of rock as it hit the cement. If I had to guess, when the lift rose again, there would be small right-angle divots in the cement—the same kind of marks we'd seen on the garage floor from earlier.

"Let me guess," I said to the guy formerly known as Josh. "You're Bill Reynolds *Junior*."

"Very good, Frank," said the bearded man. He grinned as he wheeled himself closer. "Long time no see."

The man was older, had grown a beard, and had gained some weight, but it was Bill Reynolds. Bill Reynolds Sr. The Bill Reynolds from our past.

Bill Jr. smiled. "Like I said, family is everything. Boys, meet your Moriarty."

That's when I remembered that I had seen that white van before. In the Bayport Museum parking lot.

REICHENBACH FALLS

20

JOE

COULDN'T BELIEVE IT. I HAD HITCHED A RIDE with the guy. The same guy who tried to throw my brother over the side of the dam a few years ago. I can't believe I didn't recognize him. I guess that's what the Santa Claus look will do for you. Now both Frank and I stood next to the railing with our hands up.

"I thought you were in prison," I said.

"Oh, I was," said Reynolds. He wheeled himself closer. "But I got time off for good behavior. Plus . . ." He pointed to his legs. "Special consideration for my current condition."

When Reynolds had gone over the side of the dam years ago, Frank and I had heard he had survived but with several broken bones and cracked vertebrae. No one said anything about him ending up in a wheelchair.

Frank shook his head. "We didn't know."

"How could you? I recovered from the fall," Reynolds said. "But let's just say prison hospitals aren't all they're cracked up to be. They missed a bone fragment near my spinal cord. One minute I'm working in the prison laundry, the next I'm paralyzed from the waist down."

"But you can't blame us for—" I began.

"I blame you completely," Reynolds interrupted. "And you don't know how badly I've wanted to get even with you two." He jutted a thumb at his son. "With the help of Billy here, we researched you, your friends, most of your old cases. You know, you kids with your social media make it almost too easy. Anyway, we came up with a real doozy of a plan."

"And they fell for all of it," Billy added. "Every clue, every lead. They couldn't resist." He grinned at his father. "They even created their own archnemesis."

Reynolds laughed. "Yeah, that was a hoot when I heard about this Moriarty guy. I don't read the stuff myself, but Billy's a fan."

Billy stepped closer and glanced around. "It's kind of fitting, don't you think? Since Holmes and Moriarty had their final confrontation at Reichenbach Falls."

"Yeah, but they *both* went over the falls," I said.

"And Holmes lived," Frank added. "Moriarty didn't."

Billy shrugged. "Well, those were just stories. This is reality." He leveled the pistol at us.

"I truly enjoyed torturing you two," said Reynolds Sr.

"Keeping you off guard, giving you just enough time to keep from getting arrested." He wheeled himself closer. "I thought our last setup would do the trick, you know. Everything else had gone according to plan. But looks like you were too slick to be caught by the cops. Heck, when Billy told me about the cops finding the page in your car, well, I thought we were done. But this . . ." He smiled. "This is going to be so much better."

"If you just wanted to frame us, why kill us now?" Frank asked.

Reynolds held up his hands. "Hey, I'm no killer. I just want you to go over the side there. You'll have the same chance that I had. You're both young. You might even survive."

"It was an accident," I said. "You tried to push Frank over first."

Billy snarled. "Well, now we get to finish the job, don't we?"

"Look," Frank said. "The police are on their way. Our friend told them everything we know and where we are right now. They'll be here any minute."

"Yeah," I agreed. "Why add murder to your list of crimes?"

Reynolds waved his hand dismissively. "Let 'em come. I used a remote to close the gate when we came through. You forget. These are my old stomping grounds." He gestured at his legs. "As it were. Anyway, the gate has a magnetic lock, very hard to cut through."

"Besides, after you jump, we'll be long gone," Billy added. "No one knows about Dad, and Josh Jenkins doesn't exist."

"Yeah, there's an old access road on the other side of the dam that no one remembers," said Reynolds. "We'll be out of the state before they pull your bodies out of the spillway."

"Boy, they did plan everything," I muttered.

Josh/Billy (whatever his name was) stepped forward and thrust the pistol at us. "So let's get on with it."

Frank and I turned and peered over the side. The thick torrent roared below. It splashed over the side of the dam and into the spillway below.

"I just have one more question." I looked back at our captors. "How did you get the job at the museum, Josh? Could you really have faked a resume and that much experience?"

Reynolds growled. "Stop wasting time, Hardy."

"Come on. At least let me close the case before I jump to my death."

Josh/Billy chuckled. "You two make things fun, you know that? A real flair for the dramatic. Luckily for me, Bayport Museum isn't the most high-tech of facilities. Faking a resume wasn't hard at all. Just had to create a fake LinkedIn account and email address. And I really do I have a degree in art history. They were so excited about the crime exhibit I proposed that they hired me on the spot. Lovely people. I am sorry to have broken their trust."

"Think about how sorry you'll be after our deaths. You may hate us but I don't think you want our deaths on your hands," Frank reasoned.

Reynolds leaned forward in his chair. "I bet it's real hard

to swim with a bullet in your leg." He turned to his son. "Billy, plug one of them in the leg, will ya? I'll let you pick which one."

I raised both hands. "Okay, we're going, we're going!"

Frank and I each swung a leg over the railing. Straddling the rail, we faced each other.

"Maybe if we push off hard enough," said Frank.

"We're really going to do this?" I asked.

"I don't see much of a choice," Frank said, examining the fall once again.

"Who first, huh?" Reynolds laughed. "Or both together? Hand in hand, maybe?"

Suddenly a spotlight blinded me. Frank and I each raised a hand to shield our eyes. Through squinted eyelids, I could see the police helicopter hovering above. The roar of the water had completely masked its approach.

"Billy, no!" Reynolds shouted.

Billy raised the pistol, aiming it at the helicopter.

Without a word between us, Frank and I launched ourselves off the railing. We flew *away* from the churning water and toward Billy. We hit him hard, tackling him to the ground. The pistol flew from his hand and slid across the pavement, out of the circle of light.

Billy jerked an arm free and elbowed Frank in the stomach. I heard my brother grunt as he tumbled away. That left Billy's hand free to whale on me. He punched me in the stomach, knocking the wind out of me. Before I could recover, he had jerked me to my feet and was shoving me back toward the edge. I tried to dig in, but my shoes skidded across the pavement. I scrambled to break his hold, but the day's activities had finally caught up with me. I was too weak to slow him down. We slammed into the railing and flipped over the side of the dam.

21

FRANK

JOE!" I COULD ONLY SHOUT AS I WATCHED my brother fly over the side of the dam.

I scrambled to my feet and ran after him, slamming into the railing to look down. The helicopter's spotlight illuminated the scene below. I could see my brother holding on to the lip of the dam, his expression strained. Billy's arms were wrapped around Joe's waist. The two dangled over the churning water below.

"Hang on!" I shouted as I ducked under the railing. I lay flat on the ground and reached for my brother. I grabbed his arms with both hands. Joe reached up and held tight to my wrists.

I heard sirens over the sound of the water. The police

were on their way, and they would have ropes and gear for this type of situation. Unfortunately, I could tell that my brother wouldn't hold on that long.

"Grab the post on three," I grunted. "One, two, three!"

I pulled with all my might, lifting Joe toward the handrail support post. He let go of my wrist and clamped a hand onto the post.

"I'm going to pull again," I said. "Try to lock your arm around it."

Joe gave a quick nod in reply.

I growled as I pulled. Deadlifting Joe with just my arms would be hard enough. But it took everything I had to lift the weight of both Joe and Billy. I struggled to lift my brother high enough so he could wrap his arms around the post. He grabbed his wrist with his other hand, locking himself in place.

Now, with both hands free, I went for Billy. I had to get the extra weight off my brother. He didn't look like he could hold that position much longer.

I reached down and clawed at Billy. He was locked tight on my brother, and I couldn't get a solid grip. I tried for the back of his jeans, but they were just out of reach. I didn't dare lean out farther for fear of going over myself.

The sirens were louder, but they weren't going to make it in time.

Just then I heard something beside me. I jerked my head around to see Reynolds staring me in the face. He was out of his chair and on the ground beside me. He could easily roll me over the side. I was so focused on Joe that I had forgotten about him. Once again, I was at the man's mercy.

"Save my boy, please," he pleaded. He grabbed the back of my waistband. "I can help."

Putting my trust in a criminal (and trusting that he didn't want his son to fall), I leaned way out over the edge. With Reynolds holding on to me, I was able to reach the back of Billy's waistband. "I got him!" I shouted. "Pull!"

I felt myself being dragged backward as I lifted Billy up to the edge of the dam. He let go of Joe's waist and grabbed onto another post. I heard my brother moan in relief as he shed the extra weight.

Footsteps erupted around us and hands appeared from every direction. They grabbed at Joe and Billy and lifted them completely onto the dam. Relieved, I rolled onto my back and caught my breath. I stared at the hovering helicopter, while silhouettes of police officers moved around above me.

"You okay, bro?" Joe asked.

"I'm fine," I replied. "But you're the one who decided to go for a high dive. Are you okay?"

"Oh, I think I could go to sleep right here for two days straight," Joe said.

I got to my feet. "Come on," I said as I helped my brother up. "Maybe they'll have clean sheets in our cells."

Red and blue lights flashed over the scene as police

officers led Billy away in handcuffs. Another officer followed, pushing Bill Reynolds Sr. toward the line of squad cars. A single figure emerged from the chaos and moved toward us. It was Lieutenant Wolfe.

"One thing," she said as she stopped in front of us. "I ask you not to do one thing and what's the first thing you do?"

"Uh, Lieutenant," I said.

"I don't want to hear it," she told me. "I come to your house, ask a personal favor—"

"Favor?" I asked.

"And in four days, just *four* days"—she glanced around—"I'm running a major police operation." She pointed to the sky. "We brought the helicopter. I don't know if you noticed that."

Joe raised a hand. "I . . . Thank you, ma'am."

"Hector should've told you everything that's been going on," I said.

"Oh, he did," she replied. "I almost locked him up on principle. You're just lucky that the chief called to check in. It seems that whether he likes it or not, if you two have a lead, he takes it seriously."

Joe nudged me. "Chief Olaf really does like us."

"Lieutenant, are you going to lock us up as promised?" I asked.

Lieutenant Wolfe sighed. "No, I don't suppose I will." She held up a finger. "But here's what's going to happen. I'm going to get both your statements, and when the chief returns, you're going to come in and tell him the whole thing in person." She rolled her eyes. "Because that man is not going to believe a word of my report."

"No problem," said Joe. "We can do that."

"But don't worry," said the lieutenant. "I'll make sure he reads the newspaper article *before* you come in. Get him caught up on the local events."

"Oh," Joe said.

I shook my head. This was not going to be good.

READ ON

DON'T MISS
THE NEXT HARDY BOYS ADVENTURE!

HARDY BOYS ADVENTURES #17:
THE GRAY
HUNTER'S REVENGE

JOE

THE HOUSE STOOD HIGH ON A HILL, surrounded by the skeletons of trees. Dozens of crows perched on the trees' branches, filling the silence with their harsh squawking. Frank and I stood next to the car, where he'd parked it after driving through the tall, wrought iron gates. Gates that had been kept closed for as long as anyone can remember. Closed and locked, until today.

As an amateur detective, I've been up against some crazy stuff in my time. Ruthless criminals, fiery explosions, and killer sharks to name a few. But Cliffside Manor was a whole new level of terrifying. I mean, sure, it was just a house. But the things that had supposedly happened inside that house, well . . . They were things that would keep even the bravest soul up at night.

I couldn't wait to get inside!

"You ready?" Frank asked, a chilly late-autumn breeze ruffling his dark brown hair.

I zipped up my coat against the cold and glanced back up at the house. It was constructed out of stone bricks that were almost black with age and sported a chimney on each side—one of them crumbling. Two large bay windows looked out across the estate like unblinking eyes, dark and forbidding. "I was born ready," I replied with a grin.

We started to walk toward the house, passing a dozen other parked cars on the way. "Looks like we're not the only ones coming to the estate sale," Frank observed.

I snorted. "Are you kidding me? I'm surprised the entire city isn't here. Who in their right mind would pass up the chance to go inside the hundred-year-old, superscary, super-haunted house?"

"Not Joe Hardy," Frank muttered, smirking.

"Darn right, not Joe Hardy!" I said. "Not only that; I might get to buy something belonging to one of the greatest horror writers of all time—Nathan Foxwood!"

Frank's smile fell. "It's awful about the car accident," he said. "I know you really liked his books."

"Yeah," I replied, kicking a rock across the long driveway. "I did." Not a lot of people knew about Nathan Foxwood anymore, but back in the day, he was one of the most famous authors in the world. A handful of his books had even been made into movies. When I was little, there was always a tattered Nathan Foxwood paperback on my dad's nightstand—usually with some kind of scary picture on the front and a portrait of the author himself on the back. He was a wolfish looking guy—with dark hair and a short beard and piercing eyes that seemed to bore right into you. Once I found out I was supposedly too young to read them, I promptly "borrowed" one from Dad's bedroom and hid in the closet to binge-read it with a flashlight. From then on, I was hooked.

A few years ago the news spread that Mr. Foxwood and his wife were buying the abandoned estate on the outskirts of town—the infamous Cliffside Manor. No one could understand why he'd want to live in such a terrible place—but I could. Nathan Foxwood's books were always full of the scariest things imaginable, so I figured maybe he was just trying to get some new material firsthand. I had always hoped to run into him in downtown Bayport and get to meet one of my idols, but it never happened.

And now it was too late.

Just a couple of months ago, sometime in the middle of the night, Mr. Foxwood came tearing down the hill from the manor in his car, lost control, and careened right off the side of the cliff that bordered the estate. The car burned at the bottom of the ravine for hours before anyone found out.

Rumors had been swirling ever since that Mr. Foxwood had been working on a new novel since he'd moved into town—a book about Cliffside Manor itself and its dark history. If that were true, it was a shame that he'd never get to finish it. I'd been waiting years for a new Nathan Foxwood novel.

As Frank and I approached the house, we saw a small group of people milling around near the front entrance. "Is that a reporter?" Frank asked, eyeballing a woman on the edge of the crowd holding a notepad and a camera bag. She was tall with deep brown skin and had twists of black hair cascading down her back.

"Might be," I said.

"Well, try to control yourself this time, will you?"

I rolled my eyes. I flirt with one reporter who then goes and writes an article slanted against the police, and now I'll never hear the end of it. Granted, it did cause some problems for us. As we reached the crowd, the wind picked up suddenly, and I watched as the reporter's notepad went flying out of her hands and landed at my feet.

I picked up the notepad, threw a backward glance at Frank, and shrugged. "I was totally planning on controlling myself, bro," I said. "But it looks like the universe has other ideas." I strolled over to the young woman and handed back the notepad.

"Thanks," she said with a wide smile. "Seems like the weather is conspiring to be as creepy as this house."

"Totally," I agreed. "Are you here to cover the estate sale?"

She nodded. "Aisha Best. I'm a reporter with the local newspaper. I'm actually hoping to snag an interview with Heather Foxwood—the writer's wife. I've heard that she's got quite the story about what went on in there before her husband died. No one's been able to get a hold of her since the accident, so I'm trying to get an exclusive." Aisha quirked her head at me. "What brings you here to the sale, mister . . . ?"

I sneaked a look back at Frank, who was standing a few feet away with his arms crossed, looking less than thrilled. "Umm," I said, biting my lip. "Oh, I'm just a fan, that's all. Looking to pick up some memorabilia."

Aisha raised an eyebrow, and looked like she was about to ask more questions when the front door of the manor opened. Everyone in the crowd went quiet instantly.

A wiry guy with a shaved head and copper-colored skin poked his head out of the door, his eyes roving the scene through black-rimmed glasses. He was also wearing a bow tie that seemed to be decorated with other tiny bow ties—which I thought was a little weird, but hey, it's fashion, who am I to talk? After checking his wristwatch and adjusting said bow tie, he stepped out of the house and opened his arms in welcome.

"Hello everyone," he said loudly, "and thank you for coming to the estate sale here at Cliffside Manor. My name is Adam Parker, and I'm the late Mr. Foxwood's assistant. I'm sure you're all eager to come in out of the cold, so please step inside the house, and I'll explain how all this works."

Frank and I filed in behind the rest of the crowd as they trooped though the front door. I elbowed Frank in excitement as we climbed up the stone stairs at the entryway. "We're going in! Hardly anyone has been inside this place in decades!"

Frank nodded, his eyes flashing with curiosity. "The place is probably like a time capsule. It's more than a hundred years old, you know. There might be boxes of nineteenth-century newspapers just sitting around in a basement somewhere!"

I snorted. "Bro, need I remind you that we are about to enter Cliffside Manor? As in, the most haunted house on this side of the Mississippi? And you're revving your engines over some pile of dusty newspapers?"

"Hey," Frank retorted. "At least newspapers are real. What do you expect, for some phantasm to come sailing through the walls and take a selfie with you?"

"No," I said, annoyed. Of course, when he said it that way, being so excited about the haunted aspect of the manor did seem a little silly. "Anyway," I continued as we crossed the threshold into the house, "ghosts or no ghosts, you've got to admit—this house has seen its share of sinister stuff."

Frank nodded, and I saw his eyes flick around nervously as we stepped into the front room. Legend had it that the people who'd first owned in the house, a wealthy, aristocratic family, had unknowingly built it on a piece of land belonging to a solitary man who lived in a cabin in the woods nearby. The man, who hunted deer and rabbits for food, was furious that this family had taken over and spoiled his land, but he had no legal leg to stand on, and therefore wasn't taken seriously by the family or anyone in town. The story goes that on one particular night, when a raucous dinner party filled the forest with noise and light all night, the man broke into the house carrying an ax—and left no one inside alive. Once the horrific scene was discovered, the local police pursued him into the dark forest, where he supposedly threw himself over the cliff's edge. His body was never found.

No one wanted to live in the manor after that. Gossip hung around the place like a cloud of smoke—people claimed to see the figure of the man, who they named the Gray Hunter, lurking in the shadows of the house, frightening off anyone who dared to enter. Of course, plenty of people think the whole story was nothing more than an urban legend meant to be told around a campfire, but still—just looking at the house gave you the willies.

As we entered the foyer, what I found there did nothing to dispel the idea that the place was, like, one hundred percent haunted. Heavy velvet curtains covered every window, and the only light that pierced the gloom came from a dusty chandelier above our heads. Where there wasn't creepy oil paintings of little girls and long-dead rich guys with white wigs on, the walls were covered in peeling, olive-colored wallpaper. The whole place smelled of mold, overlaid with a cloying vanilla scent that must have been sprayed around in an attempt to mask the stench of rot. It was quiet except for the ticking of a hulking grandfather clock and the wind moaning through the rafters, a sound that sent shivers down my spine.

It. Was. Awesome!

I glanced over at Frank to see if he was enjoying this as much as I was. "Isn't this great?" I asked him. "It's so creepy! I can totally imagine a Nathan Foxwood book about this place."

"The atmosphere is pretty cool," Frank admitted, studying the room. But then he wrinkled his nose. "I could do without the smell, though."

Our guide, Adam, had climbed halfway up the staircase to the second floor and was trying to get everyone's attention. "Welcome to Cliffside Manor," he said over the murmuring of the crowd. "All of the items for sale by the Foxwood estate are clearly marked with labels and suggested prices. If you are interested in purchasing an item, simply pick it up and bring it down to this room to complete the sale." He gestured toward a table where several people sat with open laptops and a cash box. "If an item is too large to carry, you can ask one of the assistants here to mark it 'sold' on your behalf. Please be courteous to other customers and . . ." Adam's voice trailed off. He looked unsure of what to say next, but finally cleared his throat and continued. "And, just be careful. As you all probably know, this is a very old house, and things can happen unexpectedly in places like these." He clapped his hands once, as if trying to clear the air of the mystery that surrounded his words. "Well! I won't take up any more of your time. Good hunting, everyone!"

People in the crowd immediately shot off in different directions, probably in search of the most valuable items on offer. "I'm going to check out the study," Frank said. "I heard that Nathan Foxwood had a ton of true crime books in his collection—I'd like to snag a few if they aren't too pricey. Where are you off to?"

I rubbed my hands together in anticipation. "I'd like to buy something if I can, but I want to do a little exploring first. Take it all in. How often do you get to just walk around a place like this?"

Frank nodded and said he'd meet back up with me in the main room in half an hour. With most of the shoppers milling around the first floor, I thought I'd get away from the pack and head upstairs. I loped up the steps two at a time until I reached the landing, where two murky hallways led away from the balcony that looked down on the foyer below. So I did what I always did when I faced a choice like this—I turned left.

The second floor of the house was no less creepy than the first—and being alone up there only upped the freaky factor tenfold. Everything was covered with a thick layer of dust, and cobwebs lurked invisibly in the air, only to be discovered by my face when I walked straight into one.

After recovering from that unpleasant, creepy-crawly sensation, I have to admit—I was starting to get a little freaked out. I kept getting this weird feeling that someone was watching me, but whenever I turned around, there was no one there.

Get ahold of yourself, Hardy! I thought. I mean, wasn't this what I wanted? A real-life haunted house experience? For all I knew, Nathan Foxwood himself had walked down these halls, getting inspiration for whatever he'd been working on before he died. I wonder if this place freaked him out, too.

As if in answer, somewhere up ahead there was an ear-splitting scream.

FRANK

BY THE TIME I GOT TO THE STUDY, IT looked like a lot of the hot ticket items had already been snatched up and the crowd had moved on. I found myself alone. The room had a high ceiling and wall-to-wall bookshelves—many of them now half-empty after being pillaged by the shoppers. Even the great mahogany desk near the window already had a SOLD sticker on it. I was surprised to see that the antique black typewriter on the desk hadn't been taken as well, but then again, it didn't have a tag, so maybe it wasn't for sale. I remember reading in Nathan Foxwood's obituary that he was infamously old-fashioned when it came to his writing—he apparently never used a computer, preferring to write his books on typewriters.

I noticed a piece of paper was still set inside the typewriter, with half a page of writing left incomplete midsentence. It was a little spooky, seeing it left behind like that, knowing that the man who had been working away at it would never get to finish the thought. I leaned over to read the words on the page, my curiosity getting the best of me.

The night was full of creeping shadows, I read, *and my heart leaped, sickeningly, at each creak of the house, at every moan across the gutters. I felt like a deer in the woods, smelling the hunter on the breath of the wind, knowing that though I still lived my fate was sealed. And then I saw him. Too large to be a living man, and too silent besides—he appeared like a devil at my bedroom door, lit from within by an unearthly glow and hefting an axe in his hands. "The Hunter," I whispered. I had scoffed at the villagers' warnings, ignored their dread tales—but I had been wrong. I hadn't believed in the Hunter, but he did not need my belief to come for my blood. I opened my mouth to—*

That was all.

Never really being interested in horror stories myself, I'd never picked one up, though Joe pushed them in my face as often as he could. But reading this now, I could see why he liked them. The words sort of grabbed you and didn't let go. Despite myself, I shivered.

And then I felt a prickle at my neck. A sensation like I was being watched. Figuring it was just another shopper who had come into the room while I was reading, I turned around to face them—but there was no one there. And then movement outside the window caught my eye, and I looked through the gauzy, threadbare curtains to see what appeared to be a figure looming on the other side. It was a large, dark shape, made featureless by the gray light behind it. I took a step closer and saw the outline of an object it seemed to be holding in its hands. A familiar object, one that glinted sharply as it moved.

An ax.

My breath caught in my throat and I stumbled back—and at that exact moment I heard the sound of a distant scream. I instinctively turned toward the sound. Did it come from upstairs? What was going on? Remembering what I'd seen, I turned back to the window, back to the dark figure—but when I looked again, it was gone.

Had I been imagining things? *Joe and his ridiculous stories are getting into my head!* I went to the window and pulled aside the curtains. Out on the balcony there was a decorative stone statue of a man—could that have been what I'd seen? Was it just a trick of the light?

That didn't matter now. Forcing myself to focus, I ran out of the room to try and find the source of the scream. Everyone in the front room was pointing upstairs, looking spooked, so I took two stairs at a time until I reached the landing.

"Joe!" I called out. "Where are you?"

"In here!" came his reply from a room at the end of the hall.

I entered the murky sitting room to find Joe kneeling down next to a woman who held one shaky hand to her head, her face ashen. She looked to be in her forties, with dark, wavy hair streaked with silver, and blue eyes that fixed on me as I came in. "I heard a scream," I said, breathless. "Is everything all right?"

"Frank," Joe began, "This is Heather Foxwood. She'd passed out when I came into the room, but she seems fine now."

"Should I call an ambulance?" I asked her.

"N-no," she managed. "I'm not ill. It's just that . . . well, I *saw* something."

"What?" I asked.

Mrs. Foxwood looked down at the floor, shaking her head. "It's impossible," she muttered to herself. "It can't be."

"Please," I urged. "Just tell us what you saw."

Mrs. Foxwood took a deep, shuddering breath before saying, "It was him. The man from the stories. The Gray Hunter."

There was a moment of silence as Joe and I let this sink in. What was she saying? That she'd seen a ghost? There had to be another explanation. Was someone playing a cruel prank on a mourning widow?

"Tell us exactly what happened," Joe encouraged her.

"I was just in here putting tickets on a few final items," she said. "When the room suddenly got colder. And then I sensed movement out of the corner of my eye—and there he was. He appeared out of nowhere, just there"—she pointed at the stone fireplace in front of us—"with an ax in his hands. He was coming toward me, soundless, when I screamed. I must have blacked out then. When I came to, though, no one was here but this young man." She gestured at Joe, who was clearly enthralled by her story.

And so I felt it was my duty to be the voice of reason in all of this.

"Mrs. Foxwood," I said. "My name is Frank Hardy, and you've already met my brother Joe. Solving mysteries is kind of a hobby of ours, so we've seen a lot of strange stuff—but they always turn out to have a logical explanation. Can you think of anyone who'd want to scare you like this? You are a local celebrity, and with what's happened, your name has been in the papers a lot over the past few days."

Mrs. Foxwood sighed. "I know what you're thinking— the grieving widow of a horror writer seeing ghosts in her house. It's almost cliché. But I am a *scientist*, Mr. Hardy. I don't have my head in the clouds like my husband did. Like you, I believe in *facts*. I believe in what I can see right in front of my eyes." She wrapped her arms around her shoulders as a shiver shook her. "And what I saw was something I cannot explain."

At that moment a bunch of people—including Adam Parker—came into the room, swarming around Heather Foxwood like buzzing bees. I pulled Joe out into the hallway, trying to get away from the chaos, but even out there people were hanging around, gossiping.

"Did you hear?" one woman was saying. "Heather Foxwood saw the Hunter!"

"Really!" said an older man with her. "I just overheard a couple other folks saying they'd seen some kind of shadowy figure lurking around as they were shopping. Looks like this place is haunted after all!"

I was rattled. Joe was overjoyed.

"It's like being in a real Nathan Foxwood novel!" he crowed.

I rolled my eyes. "You don't really think she saw a ghost, do you?" But then I suddenly remembered what I'd seen back in the study, and I felt the blood drain from my face.

Joe noticed the change in my mood immediately. "What? What's wrong?"

I shook my head. "Nothing, nothing," I said.

But my brother's like a bloodhound—once he's picked up a scent, he'll follow it until the ends of the earth. He squinted at me and exclaimed, "You saw something too, didn't you! Don't lie to me, bro—you know I can see right through you."

I crossed my arms, annoyed. "Fine! Yes, I saw something. But I'm sure there's an explanation for that too!" So I told him what I'd seen back in the study.

As I described the figure, Joe's eyes widened in amazement. "It *was* the Gray Hunter!"

"Or someone dressed up like the Gray Hunter, more like." I retorted.

"Oh, really? You said that you saw the figure only seconds before you heard Mrs. Foxwood scream. But that would have been the exact same time that *she* saw him. So tell me how this person managed to be in two places at once?"

I opened my mouth to reply, but I couldn't think of a good answer. "I don't know," I admitted. "*Yet.*"

"Excuse me," a voice broke in. Joe and I turned to see Adam Parker standing in front of us, his bow tie askew, and his eyebrows furrowed in concern. "Mrs. Foxwood tells me that you're Frank and Joe Hardy, the amateur detectives. Thank you for coming to her aid back there."

"Sure thing," I replied.

"I wonder if you would be willing to do me a favor," he continued. "I'm in a bit of a predicament here, and I'm not sure where else to turn."

Joe grinned, not even making an attempt to disguise his excitement. "Of course," he answered. "What can we do to help?"

Adam straightened his tie and launched into his story. "So, being an aspiring writer myself, getting to be Nathan Foxwood's assistant seemed like a dream come true. I could learn from the best, right? And for a while, it was like that. Mr. Foxwood was a great guy—he was always full of ideas. Until a couple of months before his death. That's when things started to fall apart. It was almost like Mr. Foxwood was losing touch with reality. I'd find him talking to himself, claiming to see things that weren't there. He heard voices. Eventually it got so bad that the night of the accident, Mrs. Foxwood was so upset about his behavior that she left to go stay with a friend for the night. I tried to talk some sense into him, but Mr. Foxwood was out of his mind. He threw me out." Adam looked at the floor. "I didn't find out about the accident until late the next day. I was in shock. Anyway, I figured that was the end of it, but then all these strange things started happening. Weird noises in the house. Whispers. Things going missing from the house. I started to think I was losing my mind too! And now all this mess at the estate sale—the reporters are already having a field day!" Adam covered his face and sighed. "Look guys, I don't believe in ghosts any more than the next person. But something *is* going on here. Mrs. Foxwood doesn't want the police involved—she's been through enough as it is—but I need to get to the bottom of this. Would you be willing to look into it for me? I don't know where else to turn."

I had to admit, the whole situation had really piqued my interest. Even if Adam hadn't asked us to take the case, not knowing the truth about what was really going on would have nagged at me for ages. When I glanced over at Joe, the dopey grin on his face told me that he was already in the game. "We'd love to help," I replied. "When do you want us to start?"

"Tonight," Adam answered. "At midnight. Mrs. Foxwood is holding a memorial for Nathan outside on the grounds. She's going to read an excerpt from the book he finished right before he died, then spread the ashes. Most of their friends and colleagues will be there, so it's the perfect opportunity for you guys to sniff around and talk to people."

Joe gave a sharp nod. "We'll be there," he said.

As we walked out of the house and back into the windy, gray day, I couldn't help but wonder who—or what—else would be joining us that night.

Looking for another great book?
Find it
IN THE MIDDLE.

Fun, fantastic books for kids
in the in-be**TWEEN** age.

IntheMiddleBooks.com

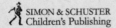